**"I'm not the naive fool
I was when we were married."**

Laura's words tumbled over themselves. "It's no concern of mine what you do, or who you do it with, but I wouldn't let Uncle Martin find out about you and his daughter. He might forget that you're an important customer and remember all the reasons he has *not* to like you."

"I doubt it." Jason's face hardened. "To him money talks. Surely you've realised that by now."

"You haven't changed," she told him bitterly. "If I were my uncle I wouldn't trust you one inch."

"Shrewd of you. You know, you should be in the Caswell boardroom dragging them back from the brink."

"Before you push them over?" she shot back at him and watched him flinch.

"Just wait and see," he said finally. "Wait and see."

Books by Sara Craven

HARLEQUIN PRESENTS

HARLEQUIN ROMANCE

These books may be available at your local bookseller.

Don't miss any of our special offers. Write to us at the following address for information on our newest releases.

Harlequin Reader Service
P.O. Box 52040, Phoenix, AZ 85072-2040
Canadian address: P.O. Box 2800, Postal Station A,
5170 Yonge St., Willowdale, Ont. M2N 6J3

SARA CRAVEN

act of betrayal

Harlequin Books

TORONTO • NEW YORK • LONDON
AMSTERDAM • PARIS • SYDNEY • HAMBURG
STOCKHOLM • ATHENS • TOKYO • MILAN

Harlequin Presents first edition November 1985
ISBN 0-373-10832-X

Original hardcover edition published in 1985
by Mills & Boon Limited

Printed in U.S.A.

CHAPTER ONE

THE traffic was heavy all the way, but that was how it always turned out when you were in a hurry, Laura thought, drumming her fingers impatiently on the steering wheel.

She was running late already, but perhaps the meeting at the works would go over time. It was certainly important enough to do so.

She glanced at her watch, with a brief sigh. She wished Uncle Martin had given her more notice, but from his secretary's agitated call, she'd gathered he'd had very little warning himself. And supplying delicious lunches for important clients at the works was part of her job, as well as a challenge, so she couldn't complain. Besides, she remembered herself drily, clients rarely came quite as important as Tristan Construction.

The traffic lights changed, and she let in the clutch and drove on towards the industrial estate where Caswell Carpets had their main works and offices.

She ran through the menu in her mind as she drove. Watercress soup to start, followed by pheasant in a red wine sauce, all plucked from the freezer and packed in cartons in the boot. To follow, the strawberries she'd just collected from the local market garden served with crème Chantilly.

She hoped the Tristan directors would be suitably impressed. She also wished they'd chosen some other day for their visit. She'd had plans of her own, including a visit to the hairdressers, she thought, giving herself a swift disparaging glance in the driving mirror. She could probably have managed it too if Celia had only agreed to give her a hand with the lunch, but she had learned a long time ago that her cousin's model-girl prettiness concealed a selfishness which more than matched the charm she worked at so determinedly.

Clad in brief shorts and a minimal suntop, Celia had been bound for the garden to sunbathe, and she'd refused, smilingly but totally, to accompany Laura to the works instead.

'Honestly, sweetie, I'd be less than useless,' she'd protested. 'That microwave oven you persuaded Daddy to install frightens me to death. Anyway, you were only going to have your hair trimmed, and you can do that any time.'

'Of course,' Laura said without irony. 'I just thought you might want to help, as there's a panic on.'

Celia waved a languid hand. 'There's always a panic on.'

'Perhaps,' Laura said rather drily. 'But this time it's Tristan Construction.'

'Am I supposed to know who they are?'

Laura gave her a resigned look. 'I think you should,' she said crisply. 'They're only the customers who could stop Caswells sliding any further into the red this year. They've got two major building projects in this area—offices and flats—and the carpeting contracts are up for grabs. Naturally, your father wants first grab.'

Celia's lack of concern about the fluctuating fortunes of the company never ceased to surprise her. Or was her cousin deliberately closing her eyes to the present difficulties Caswells was suffering, she wondered. Celia didn't like unpleasant facts, and never had. To her Caswells was as firm and unshakable as the Rock of Gibraltar, and she preferred to ignore the fact that other companies, many of them older established than Caswells, and leaders in their fields, had gone to the wall in the present recession.

Laura supposed her cousin couldn't wholly be blamed. She had always been encouraged to think of herself as a rich man's daughter. Uncle Martin had indulged her since the day she was born, and the only thing she had done since leaving school that even approached work was redesigning the interior decor of the large house they all lived in. Celia's tastes leaned towards the opulent, to Laura's regret, but Uncle Martin regarded his home as a showcase for the company, and seemed well pleased with her efforts.

'Then I hope he gets it,' Celia yawned. 'Feed them well, won't you, darling. Oh—and Laurie, you will change, won't you? Put on something decent?'

'I don't actually wait on table, you know.' Laura felt a little curl of anger deep inside her, as she glanced down at her simple denim skirt and short sleeved top. 'I'm not on public display to the customers. I spend all my time in the kitchen.'

Celia gave a graceful shrug. 'Just as you please. But isn't it enough to behave like a drudge? You really don't have to look like one as well.'

Her words still rankled with Laura as she turned into Caswells main gate, returning the salute from the security man.

She knew she was being a fool to allow it, especially when she should be inured to Celia's little ways by now, and particularly when her affection and gratitude to her uncle made her suffer them in silence anyway. He had been endlessly kind to her, giving her a home during that most difficult part of her young life when her parents had been killed in a motor crash in France.

And later, when her life fell apart again, he'd helped her to pick up the pieces, and she would always be grateful for that. Always. And if it meant tolerating Celia's waspishness and selfishness, then she would do so.

Nevertheless, she had changed into a neat navy cotton shirtwaister, despising herself for doing it even as she fastened the buttons.

She pulled into the executives' car park, and braked, swearing mildly under her breath. She had no official parking space, but a place was always left for her, and today it was occupied by a long sleek Jaguar.

Laura, staring frustratedly at it through the wind-screen, supposed it must belong to one of the Tristan directors. She didn't recognise it anyway, and now she had to resign herself to driving round to the rear of the building, and taking all the food up the stairs to the boardroom floor, instead of using the reception lift, and the brawny arms of George the commissionaire.

It was fast turning out to be one of those days, she decided ruefully.

It took three journeys, and she was flushed and a little breathless as she unpacked her cartons and switched on the oven, and checked unobtrusively that the waitresses had laid the dining room table correctly.

She'd hulled and washed the strawberries, and was layering them in a glass bowl with the crème Chantilly, when the kitchen door almost burst open, and Mrs Ferguson, her uncle's secretary came in at the run.

'Oh, you're here.' Fergie looked more flushed than Laura did herself, and sounded agitated. 'So you didn't get the message. I was afraid of that. I should have 'phoned myself—made sure.'

Laura gave her a long look. 'I hope you haven't been at the boardroom sherry, Fergie,' she suggested mischievously. 'You did speak to me, you know. That's why I'm here.'

'Oh, no, not that.' Fergie shook her head, looking more distressed than ever. 'You see, there was another message—later. Your uncle told them to call you from reception, but I was certain you'd already have left. I did try to tell him . . . Oh dear, it's all so difficult . . .'

'Don't tell me,' Laura said resignedly. 'Tristan Construction are all vegetarians.'

'What?' Fergie gulped and stared.

'Allergic to strawberries?' Laura went on, frowning a little. 'Or simply not turned up?'

'No, they're here. That's the trouble. You see, we didn't know—how could we—until they arrived. And then it was too late.'

Fergie looked as if she was about to burst into tears, and Laura could hardly believe what she was seeing. Mrs Ferguson was one of the mainstays of the company, and under normal circumstance totally unflappable. What in the world could have got her in this state?

She gave her an encouraging smile. 'It can't be that bad,' she urged gently. 'Surely they're not international terrorists holding Uncle Martin to ransom for the formula of the new miracle fibre? Don't worry about a thing. I'll poison the soup.'

But Fergie was almost wringing her hands. 'Oh, Laura,' she wailed. 'Their managing director—it's Jason Wingard—your ex-husband.'

Laura found she was putting the bowl of cream she was holding very carefully down on to the table. It was suddenly important to move slowly and certainly, and to wait to speak too, until she was sure she could trust her voice.

She said, 'There must be some mistake. Jason was—was an artist. He doesn't know anything about the building trade. And Tristan Construction is a big company. Besides—his name would have been on the letterheads. Uncle Martin—one of you would have seen it.'

She was building up excuses like a wall to shelter behind, because it just couldn't be possible for Jason to walk back into her life like this. She hadn't seen or heard anything of him for over three years now. He'd simply touched the edge of her life like a comet, a star of ill-omen, then vanished, leaving her emotionally scorched, hardly able to believe what had happened to her. She'd prayed she would never have to set eyes on him again. And now, out of the clearest of blue skies—this.

Fergie shook her head. 'It was the first thing I checked, but there was only the company heading, plus the address and telex. No directors' names at all. Your uncle told reception to 'phone you at once—to stop you coming here—or to turn you back downstairs if you'd already left. They must have missed you somehow.'

Laura said, 'The car park was full.' She took a deep breath, marshalling all her forces determinedly. 'It's kind of my uncle to be so concerned, but I can cope, truly I can. I'm here now, and I'll prepare the lunch as I always do. I don't have to see—Jason, and he need never even know I'm around.' She made herself smile. 'No problem.'

'Are you quite sure?' Fergie gave her a harrassed look, then glanced at her watch. 'I'll have to go. I'll let your uncle know what you've decided.' She shuddered. 'Oh, dear, he was so angry. I've never seen him in such a state. I was terrified he might have a heart attack.'

Laura looked down at the strawberries. She said neutrally. 'He and Jason—they never liked each other. Never got on.'

Their mutual antagonism, she remembered, had been the first shadow across the dazzling glitter of her happiness. Too bright, too dazzling, like a day in spring which promises sunlight, but ends in weeping rain.

Fergie said, 'Oh dear,' again, rather helplessly. Then, 'Don't even attempt to clear away afterwards. I'll have it all seen to. Just do what needs to be done, then get away.'

'I'll do exactly that.' Laura made her tone reassuring, and Fergie gave her an uncertain smile and dashed away.

Laura was alone again, and she stood for a long moment, forcing herself to breathe deeply and calmly, regaining her equilibrium. She'd told Fergie she could cope, but she wasn't altogether sure it was true.

It was all so unexpected—so frankly incredible.

They'd parted in bitterness, and Jason hadn't contested the divorce, although her solicitor had said that was often the case where there were no children to fight over. She could still remember her reaction to that—the swift agonised sob, and the way he'd looked at her, kind but uncomprehending. But that had been the only time she'd come near breaking point, on the surface at least.

There had been no communication between Jason and herself—none at all, and she'd been thankful for it—thankful there was no need for maintenance payments or property settlements. 'A clean break' her uncle had called it, and that was what it had been. Only it was more like a cut than a break—an amputation, where the aching continued long after the severance had healed.

So why had Jason chosen to probe the wound again? Because that was what he was doing. True, he could not have expected to find her at the works, but he must know that news of his reappearance would get back to her sooner or later.

Surely it wasn't his intention to torment her by turning up in her life at intervals, when least expected? That would be too cruel, she thought numbly, but after all, Jason specialised in cruelty. Wasn't she only too aware of that?

She could serve the lunch and run. That was the easy bit. The hard part would come later—closing him out of her mind, as she thought she'd succeeded in doing already, refusing to allow herself any more fruitless speculations about the reasons for his presence at the works, or his intentions.

All her cookery school training was needed, as the moment approached when the meal would be served.

Laura found herself wishing she'd not made it so easy for herself—that she'd decided to splurge with some complicated dish which needed every atom of concentration of which she was capable. She was on edge all the time, keyed up for the sound of voices, even though she knew it was doubtful whether they would penetrate so far. Quite deliberately, the kitchen had been planned at a discreet distance from the board's dining room, and she was thankful for this as never before, because as soon as the food was served she could leave the way she had come, with no-one being any the wiser.

She was just frying the croutons for the soup when the waitresses arrived, and as Laura poured the fragrant soup into the two matching tureens, she wondered if they knew who was waiting to be served in the dining room—if word had got around somehow? She hoped not. They were excellent workers, but she knew from past experience that they loved a good gossip, and she had no wish to be the butt of any sidelong glances, or murmured remarks.

But, she reminded herself, she was probably being over-sensitive. It was doubtful whether more than the merest handful of people at Caswells knew she had been married, let alone her former husband's name. She'd got married in London, after all, not locally, and most of her brief married life had been spent in the capital too.

'Well, they've got good appetites, I'll say that for them.' One of the girls came back with the first batch of used plates. 'All except Mr Martin, that is,' she added. 'He hardly touched a drop of his soup.' She gave Laura a confidential wink. 'And they're not the usual collection of stuffed shirts either. There's one there I could fancy myself.'

Laura's heart jerked uneasily, but all she said was, 'Be careful of the casserole dishes. They're very hot.'

'They look a real treat.' The girl began to load the

bowls of croquette potatoes, green beans, buttered baby carrots and creamed broccoli on to her tray.

Laura smiled non-committally, and began to stack the soup plates into the dish washer. Like most good cooks, she enjoyed having her efforts praised, and savoured, but not today. Today, she just wanted this particular lunch over and done with so she could make good her escape.

She wandered about restlessly, measuring coffee into the filter machine, filling cream jugs and sugar basins, endlessly arranging and re-arranging a dish of home made petits fours.

The meal was only a prelude, she knew. Her uncle had often declared that the real business was done over coffee, brandy and a good cigar afterwards when everyone was relaxed and replete, and Laura made sure always that the coffee was strong, aromatic and plentiful, just as he liked it.

She was chafing inwardly, wanting to serve the dessert and the cheese. Once that was done, she could go. The girls could manage anything that remained, between them.

The kitchen window was open and she had the extractor fan in operation, but she could still feel beads of perspiration on her forehead.

For heaven's sake, she adjured herself sharply, calm down. It's awkward and embarrassing, but it isn't the end of the world.

But it was once, a sly voice whispered in her mind, when you realised the kind of man you had married. When it all came crashing down round your naïve, idealistic ears. That was the end of the world—or it seemed so.

But she was older now. Three years older, and three years wiser, please God. She wasn't a stupid trusting child any more and she supposed she had Jason to thank for that.

And she also had him to thank for the fact that these kitchen walls seemed to be closing in on her like a prison. She was almost counting the tiles, when the girls came bustling back.

'There's a funny atmosphere in there,' one of them informed her, jerking a head in the direction of the dining room. 'Important meeting is it?'

'All orders are important these days.' Laura scraped the pheasant bones into the waste disposal. There were enough rumours flying round Caswells already about the company's difficulties, without her adding to them, but it was no secret the sales department had had long faces for months. Uncle Martin had great hopes of Tristan Construction—until now.

She saw the waitresses back to the dining room with their final loads, and relaxed slightly. It was nearly over.

The coffee was filling the room with its fragrance, when she heard the slight squeak of the kitchen door as it opened.

Without looking round, she said, 'I'm going now, but I've left everything else ready.'

'So I see,' Jason remarked. 'You're a domestic paragon, my sweet, but then you always were.'

Laura had been reaching for her bag. Shock made her jerk nervously at the strap, and the bag fell, disgorging its contents at her feet. For a moment, she stared down at them blank-faced, as if she'd never seen them before, then moving like an automaton, she turned to face him.

He was lounging in the doorway, hands thrust into the pockets of an expensively cut dark suit. It occurred to her as she stared at him that she'd never seen Jason in a suit before—not even on their wedding day. He'd always dressed casually in the extreme—denims and sweaters usually. This new conventionality was a shock, until she looked more closely, and saw that the silk tie had been loosened impatiently, and the top button of the pristine white shirt left unbuttoned. The thick unruly mane of dark hair had been trimmed, but not tamed, and still hung nearly to his collar. The lines of the thin, clever, arrogant face were deeper and more harsh, and the eyes which met hers were as bleak and inimical as they had been at their last confrontation.

No, she thought. He might wear the trappings of convention, but underneath he was still as dangerous as ever.

He said silkily, 'Are you going to tell me I've changed?'

'I don't think it would be true.' She was amazed to hear how normal her voice sounded. 'What are you doing here?'

'I'm here on business. Don't pretend you didn't know.' His mouth curled sardonically. 'I saw all the agitated fluttering when I walked in. And I don't need to ask why you're here, of course. You're still a superlative cook, Laura, even though kind Uncle Martin is reaping the benefit now instead of me.'

She went down on one knee, and began to shovel her things back into her bag, her fingers clumsy with haste.

'You've missed this.' Jason bent too and handed her a slender gilt scent spray.

'Thanks.' She almost snatched it from him.

'Relax, Laura.' There was a note of warning in his voice, steely and implacable. 'Our paths are bound to cross during the next few months, so the best thing you can do is accept it.'

'And if I'm not prepared to do that?' She gave him a bitter look. 'I meant what I said, Jason—that I never wanted to see you again. I still mean it. So why are you tormenting me like this?'

'Had it been left to me,' he said gently, 'I would not have come within a hundred miles of this bloody place. But these are hard times, darling, and most companies get work where they can and are glad of it. Tristans is no exception. Under the circumstances, the risk of offending your delicate sensibilities had to be discounted. I hope that precious little ego of yours will survive?'

She took a deep breath. 'So—it's all a coincidence. But the carpeting for all these units you plan to build didn't have to come from Caswells. You could have stayed away from here.'

'And we still might,' Jason said bitingly. 'We have other firms to see besides this one. No orders have been placed, or contracts signed—yet.'

'We shan't be going on our knees to you.' The palms of her hands felt damp, and she had to resist an impulse to run them betrayingly down her skirt.

'Oh, I'm sure that goes for you, my sweet, and possibly your uncle. But not his fellow directors. They're gratifyingly eager to do business with us—even to the extent of rushing this new wonder fibre of yours into production.' He looked round him rather grimly. 'Perhaps you should come out of your cosy little kitchen occasionally, and see what's happening in the real world.'

'Thanks, but I think I know,' she said tautly. She had her bag firmly gripped now, but he was still blocking her path. 'Will you excuse me please? I—I have to go . . .'

'Why?' he asked. 'We've confronted each other at last, and neither of us has been turned to stone, so why run away?'

'I'm not running,' she denied hastily. 'But I do have other things to do—a hairdressing appointment for one . . .'

'Ah.' His grey eyes gave one swift disparaging glance at the tawny hair, pulled back from her face and confined at the nape of her neck, for coolness and ease while she was working, by an elastic band. 'It's time you abandoned the schoolgirl look, Laura. You're a grown-up lady now. Or doesn't marriage and divorce confer any kind of maturity?' He ignored her infuriated gasp, and went on. 'But I'm sure you can spare a moment or two from your crowded schedule to join us in the boardroom for coffee. My colleagues want to congratulate you on the meal.'

'That's kind of them, but I prefer to take it as read.' Laura took another shaky breath. 'You say our paths have to cross. Jason. Well I don't believe that's necessary at all. If today could be cancelled, then I'd wipe it out without a second thought.'

'Not very civilised of you, darling.'

'I don't feel particularly civilised,' Laura snapped. 'And don't call me that.'

He lifted one shoulder in a shrug. 'What would you prefer to be called then? Mrs Wingard?'

'No.' The small sound was expelled from her in a kind of agony. 'Not that—ever again. The first thing I did when the decree was made final was revert to my maiden name.'

'How said for you that it can only be in name,' he said softly. He looked at her bare left hand. 'All traces of me removed except one. Did you sell your ring for scrap?'

'I gave it to Oxfam.' It was a lie. She'd considered that, but in the end, she'd hidden it at the bottom of her trinket drawer. It was a decision she hadn't been able to rationalise even at the time, and the last thing she wanted was to have to think about it again now.

'Very public spirited of you,' he approved sardonically, and she felt a dull flush rise in her cheeks. 'What a pity you can't dispose of me quite so easily.'

'I thought I had,' Laura said shortly. She lifted her chin. 'I'd like to leave now please. And I imagine those colleagues of yours will be starting to wonder where you are.'

He grinned suddenly, and she felt tension break out all over her like porcupine quills. 'I'm sure kind Uncle Martin will enlighten them. He was even less pleased to see me than you are if that's possible.'

'And that surprises you?'

'No,' Jason said. 'But then there's very little about the Caswell family that could surprise me any more.' He moved, straightening his shoulders, and Laura felt herself recoil. He saw it, and stopped, the grey eyes narrowing glacially as they surveyed her. 'But I still seem to have the ability to surprise you,' he said half to himself. 'How interesting. Perhaps some further research is called for.'

She said hoarsely, reading his purpose in his face, 'You dare lay one finger on me, and . . .'

'You'll do what? Scream for your uncle?' He shook his head slowly. 'Not this time, darling. He's too busy chasing a contract to hear you.' As he spoke, he walked forward, until he was only inches away from her. There was a row of units right behind her, and nowhere to retreat to. Besides, it suddenly seemed a matter of honour to stand her ground, as if this unwanted proximity didn't concern her one bit, although her breathing had become painful and even difficult.

Jason's hand touched the nape of her neck, his fingers stroking the smooth skin. Her mouth went dry, and her hands clenched into fists at her sides.

'This thing,' Jason said softly, 'is an obscenity.' The elastic band was tugged from her hair, not gently, and the soft tawny strands fell round her face. It was all she could do not to cry out. She found herself wondering absurdly where the waitresses had got to. Surely they would be back at any moment. Surely . . .

She'd cried a lot of tears and spent many sleepless nights, trying to forget how it had once been between Jason and herself, and she thought she had succeeded.

Now, the first seeking warmth of his mouth on hers

told her that she was wrong, and every fibre of her being whimpered in shock.

She stood rigidly, resisting the practised sensual teasing of his mouth, the warm coaxing of his tongue against the unrelenting contours of her lips. Pain armoured her against response, and she was grateful for it, because it could have been so tempting to let the past slide away, and with it the icy restraint she'd imposed on herself.

Sex was the great betrayer. It made your body impose on your mind. It robbed you of reason and commonsense. It made you believe there could be 'happy ever after', and Laura wanted no more of it.

But she wasn't prepared for this gentleness in him, and it bewildered her. She almost wished he'd shown her some of the brutality of their last time together. It would have provided a focus for her hatred, for her disgust.

This insidious probing at her senses was less easy to fight, and it made her afraid, because the memories it evoked were not of anger or bitterness and accusation, but of their early days together, and all the promise of them.

A promise which Jason had cynically and blatantly broken. That was what she had to remember—all she had to remember. Nothing else mattered—no laughter-filled days, or passion-warmed nights. No moments when she'd wondered crazily why she'd been chosen to be so lucky.

Because ultimately and heartbreakingly, there'd been no luck about it. She was simply Laura Caswell, a girl who had been married for her money. Not the first one to find herself in that situation, and certainly not the last.

The thoughts ran wildly in her brain, bolstering her against the first slow, sweet stirring of the senses which Jason's kiss was inevitably arousing. He'd taught her to want him, to want the pleasure which his mouth and hands and body could give her, and her starved sexuality was slowly, almost incredulously reviving under the insistent pressure of his lips against hers. She wanted to open her mouth, to sink against his body, and feel the hard possession of his arms round her again. She wanted it so much that she ached inside—an ache which pleaded for assuagement . . .

With a little cry, she jerked her head back, bringing up a clenched fist to scrub furiously at her lips. 'You're disgusting.'

'You think so?' he asked mockingly. 'Where have you spent the last three odd years, Laura? In a nunnery?'

'That's none of your business.' How dare he stand there so utterly unmoved, when her heart was threatening to choke her with its hammering. 'And may I remind you that you've lost the legal right to—maul me.'

He shrugged. 'Merely an experiment, darling. Nothing to get hysterical about.' He laughed briefly. 'And there wasn't, was there? It's all quite dead. Not a single pang of unrequited passion on either side. So— no reason why we can't behave civilly to each other when we meet from now on—as we inevitably will. *Shake hands forever. Cancel all our vows.* Isn't that how it goes?'

He paused. 'We may never be friends, Laura, but we have to be acquaintances. You can surely see that?'

There was another, longer pause, as if he was waiting for some kind of reaction, perhaps even an answer to what he had said.

Then he added, 'Anyway—think about it.'

He turned, the door gave its familiar monitory squeak, and Laura was alone.

CHAPTER TWO

THERE was a lay-by about half a mile from the factory complex. Laura drove the car into it, and stopped, slumping limply forward over the driving wheel.

She'd left Caswells at the run, uncaring about who might see her, or what conclusions might be drawn. She'd fumbled with the ignition, crashed the gears, and missed the concrete gatepost at the exit by a whisker.

It was a miracle she'd got this far without an accident, only she'd stopped believing in miracles. They were on a par with the tooth fairy, who'd stopped calling a very long time ago.

She sat very still, her hands still gripping the wheel as she sought to control the deep inner trembling which threatened to convulse her.

She kept hoping she would wake up and find it had all been just another nightmare—trying, but purely transitory—but she knew that however many times she might pinch herself, Jason was not going to vanish like a bad dream this time.

He was there. He was flesh and blood, and for one endless, searing moment, he'd made her feel like flesh and blood too.

She groaned, nausea rising in her throat, and sat up slowly, fighting her own self-disgust.

How could she have felt like that—even for a second? She knew what Jason was—who better? she thought bitterly—so what in the name of God had she been doing to allow him anywhere near her?

She lay back in her seat, staring sightlessly through the windscreen.

Well, it had happened, and while it was shaming to

realise just how close her body had been to betraying her, the situation wasn't totally irretrievable.

Because Jason had not guessed. She repeated the words aloud to herself, giving each one its own resounding emphasis—because it mattered. It really did.

She'd been a total innocent when they'd first met, but under his tutelage she'd blossomed, discovering depths in her nature, aspects of sexuality which she'd never dreamed existed. Jason was the first man to whom she'd been physically attracted, the first one to teach her sensual delight. It was hardly surprising that she'd imagined she was in love with him, or that she'd been naïve enough to believe that he loved her in return.

She'd soon learned differently, of course—even before that first, crazy, delirious year had wound to a close.

'Trust me,' he'd urged. 'Laura, trust me please.'

I trusted him, she thought. I'd have done anything for him. I'd have followed him naked, if he'd asked me. Only he never asked.

She hadn't let herself cry much during the long months while she was waiting to be divorced. She hadn't cried a great deal since, but there were tears now. Laura put her hands over her face and sobbed. The moisture ran between her splayed fingers, and down the backs of her hands. She could hear herself moaning, and the desolation of the sound frightened her into silence, and ultimately into control again.

There was a box of tissues in the car, and she used them to blot the worst signs of her emotional collapse from her face. She didn't want to have to face Celia with red eyes, and a blotched skin. In fact, it occurred to her, she would prefer not to have face Celia at all just yet.

She sat for a moment, drumming her fingers restlessly on the steering wheel, then started the car with new determination. She would go to Alan's house—take him up on one of the many invitations she'd always steered clear of in the past.

After all, she liked Alan, she argued defensively to herself. She'd enjoyed their dates together over the past year, but she'd been wary of allowing their relationship to develop along more intimate lines, and when Alan had shown signs of trying to force the pace a little, she'd always drawn back. One day she might be ready for a serious involvement again, but that day had not yet arrived.

And although to seek him out like this might not be altogether fair to Alan in view of the ambivalence of her feelings, it was necessary. She needed the reassurance of his undoubted regard for her. He was the present tense in her life. Jason was the past.

It took Laura just under ten minutes to drive out of town to the small village where he lived. One minute there were suburban houses and neat gardens, and then, as abruptly as if someone had drawn a line, there were fields and trees and narrow lanes, with fingerposts pointing out the hidden life of the countryside.

She parked her car on the verge opposite his small cottage, and crossed the lane to the gate, returning the friendly nod she received from an elderly man working in the neighbouring garden.

As she walked up the path, she could hear the sound of Alan's typewriter clicking away through the open window, and she hesitated for a moment before knocking at the door.

Alan had trained originally as a teacher, but because of the cuts in education spending, he'd never managed to secure a permanent post in an English department anywhere. So, instead, he'd turned to freelance writing, and was managing to make an adequate living if not an affluent one, eked out by some private coaching. Among other things, he wrote a restaurant column for the local paper, as well as being its drama critic, and in a way it was through this column that they'd become friends, because when they'd been casually introduced at a party, Laura had told him bluntly she didn't always agree with his praise or criticism of the local eating houses, and they'd enjoyed discussing their differing opinions.

It was clear he was working now, and she was unwilling to disturb him for such purely selfish reasons, but just as she was preparing to turn away, he called, 'Come in, Laura. The door isn't locked.'

He met her in the tiny hall, smiling delightedly. 'Hey—this is fantastic. I was just going to 'phone you. What brings you this way?'

'Oh, I was just passing.' She hated lying, and was bad at it. 'Could I use the bathroom, do you suppose?'

'Of course,' he said briskly. 'It's on the right at the top of the stairs. And I'll make some coffee.'

As she made hurried repairs to the ravages which emotion had done to her face, Laura wondered wryly whether Alan had seen she was upset, but been too tactful to enquire about it. On balance, she decided the dimness of the light in the hall had probably been to her advantage, and he hadn't noticed a thing. She hoped not, anyway. She didn't want to have to embark on lengthy explanations.

He was emerging from the kitchen with a tray as she came downstairs, and she followed him into a sizeable, cluttered living room. There was a large desk under the window, and a frankly sagging sofa in front of the empty fireplace, flanked by a couple of easy chairs which had also seen better days.

But for all that, the room had a cosy welcoming air, which in Laura's view, the Caswell mansion totally lacked.

The coffee was good too. Alan was fussy about the blends he chose, and it showed. She accepted the pretty pottery beaker he handed her with a murmured word of thanks.

He perched on the arm of a chair, smiling eagerly. 'I'm glad I didn't 'phone and find you out. I get the impression your uncle's housekeeper doesn't altogether appreciate taking messages from me.'

Laura smiled rather ruefully. 'It's no fault of yours. I'm afraid that she resents me. She's been with the family for years, and my uncle thought I could take some of the housekeeping burdens off her shoulders, but she doesn't see it that way at all. Anyway, why did you want to speak to me?'

'I've been asked to cover the opening of a brand-new restaurant in Burngate tonight,' he said. '*The Echo* were going to send Linda Watson from staff, because there'll be free champagne, but as she's gone down with some virus they've had to fall back on me.' He gave a self-deprecating grin. 'I'm allowed to take guests, so I wondered if you'd go with me?'

In any other circumstances, Laura thought she would probably have made an excuse. It didn't sound like her sort of junket at all, but tonight the last thing she wanted to do was sit at home and brood.

She said lightly, 'It sounds like fun. Pick me up early, and have a drink with us first.'

His face lit up. 'I'd really like that.' He paused. 'Your family don't object to you going out with a struggling hack?'

'Is that how you see yourself?' Laura asked. She gave a faint shrug. 'Why should they object? I'm not a child anymore. I have my own life to live.'

'I suppose so.' He spoke slowly, as if measuring his words. 'But do you live it? I mean—you seem so sheltered sometimes.'

'I assure you I don't feel it,' she told him drily. 'But if you're nervous of my ivory tower, we could always meet in a bar.'

'Oh, no,' he denied hastily. 'I'd like to meet your uncle.'

He didn't actually say 'at long last' but his tone implied it, and Laura bit her lip. Clearly her attempts to keep their relationship on a strictly casual basis hadn't been as subtle as she'd hoped, and now Alan was taking her decision to introduce him into the family circle as a step towards a greater intimacy. She could only hope she wasn't starting something she'd be unable to control.

She'd never told Alan any details about her personal life. To him, she was just Laura Caswell, and he had no idea there had ever been a Laura Wingard. It had never seemed necessary to tell him, but now it occurred to her that she was going to have to, and she wondered how he would react.

He said suddenly, 'Where do you go to, Laura?'

Her eyes flicked questioningly to his face. 'What do you mean?'

'I'm not even sure myself. It's just sometimes when we're together, you seem to—vanish—somewhere inside yourself. It makes me wonder.' He laughed rather awkwardly. 'Perhaps it's just that I'm not very exhilarating company.'

Her glance held compunction. Obviously, he needed reassurance too. 'It certainly isn't that,' she said gently. 'I don't think I even realise I'm doing it.'

There was a pause, then he said, 'If you've got problems, it can help sometimes to share them.' He sounded tentative, unsure, as if aware he was offering himself in a new role, and she was grateful, even if she couldn't be sure it was what she wanted from him.

She drank down her coffee, and rose. 'If we're going on the town, then I'd better do something about my appearance. I don't want to put my fellow revellers off their food.'

'You'd never do that,' he protested.

She knew that he wanted to kiss her, and she made herself yield as he took her in his arms, hoping that the touch of his lips would turn her to fire, totally erasing the memory of that other devastating kiss.

Oh, Alan, forgive me, she thought remorsefully, as her hands slid up to clasp his shoulders in the simulation of passion. She felt his arms tighten round her in response, his mouth move on hers with growing confidence. Laura closed her eyes, waiting, praying for the alchemy to happen. After all, he was young, he was attractive in a quiet way, and she wanted to want him. She wanted another man to kindle the deep flame in her body which Jason had always lit so effortlessly.

Since their parting, she'd been in a kind of limbo, leading a half-life, but now she wanted to be whole again, and Alan could be the man to make her so.

But once again, there were no miracles. The kiss was pleasant, but it ignited no fierce, answering excitement within her, and it was a relief when he let her go— reluctantly, but without initiating any further intimacies.

There was tenderness in his face when he looked at her, and a slight triumph as well, which she supposed was understandable. She'd never invited caresses in the past, and she'd always been the first to draw back.

He said huskily, 'Well, I'll see you later then,' and Laura tried not flinch at the new possessive note in his voice.

She said steadily, 'I'm looking forward to it,' and wished with all her heart that it could be true.

Celia was nowhere to be seen when she got back to the house, her lounger in the garden unoccupied, a discarded magazine tossed on the grass beside it, and an empty jug which had once contained orange juice still reposing with its used glass on a wrought iron table nearby. Laura put the lounger away in the summer-house, and carried the other things across the lawn towards the house.

She was almost at the french windows which opened

into the drawing room, when she heard Celia laughing, the low throaty chuckle which meant there was a man about.

Her cousin was entertaining one of her numerous boyfriends, Laura decided resignedly. If it was Greg Arnold, she could only hope he would save his more risque stories until she was out of the room.

She was almost tempted to retrace her steps, and go in by the kitchen entrance, but she told herself forcefully not to be so silly.

She was actually inside the room, with retreat impossible, when she saw the man sharing the wide sofa with Celia was Jason.

'Hello, sweetie,' Celia flashed her a smile. She'd thrown on the shirt which matched her sunbathing gear, but she still managed to look alluringly undressed. She waved a hand at Jason. 'I gather introductions aren't necessary.' She giggled. 'What an amazing surprise for you both. I always understood Laura's ex-husband was a struggling artist, and now he turns up as a tycoon. You sly thing, Laura, keeping it all to yourself like this.'

Before Laura could speak, Jason intervened smoothly. 'She can hardly be held responsible for not telling you I was the boss of Tristan Construction. She didn't know it herself until a few hours ago.'

'So it was all your little secret?' Celia's eyes fastened limpidly on his face. 'Perhaps you should have told her. You might both still be living in connubial bliss.'

'I doubt that.' His lips smiled, but the words bit. 'In any case, I'm sure there are far more interesting subjects to discuss than my past matrimonial difficulties.'

Celia pouted a little. 'Are there any current ones?'

'No.' He didn't look at Laura at all. 'So far, I've decided not to risk another dip in the troubled waters of marriage.' He looked at her ringless left hand. 'It seems like a view we share.'

Celia shrugged gracefully. 'I was engaged—once, but

to be honest I find the whole concept of marriage the teeniest bit cramping and old-fashioned, even though the divorce laws have made things easier.'

Laura listened with a sense of incredulity. Easier, she thought helplessly. Easier? Was that really how Celia regarded those few brief moments in court which tore apart flesh and sinew and emotion?

She said in a small wooden voice, 'Well, if you'll excuse me I'll just take these things to the kitchen.'

'And while you're there, sweetie, you might see about some tea for us.' Celia's tone was casual, but the words, putting Laura in a position of subservience was quite deliberate.

Hot outrage rose in Laura's throat. She was sorely tempted to yell, 'Get your own damned tea,' and brain Celia with the empty jug for good measure, but she exercised an almost superhuman restraint.

She returned coolly, 'Of course.' She looked at Jason, lifting her brows enquiringly, 'Milk or lemon?'

His mouth twisted. She saw a glimmer of anger deep down. 'You mean you don't remember?' he asked silkily. 'I think lemon on such a warm day—don't you?'

It didn't make a particle of difference what she thought, Laura told herself as she left the room. She had no intention of sharing the tea with them, and watching Celia exercise her blatant wiles on Jason.

The kitchen was full of delicious baking smells, and Mrs Fraser, looking harassed was removing a tray from the oven.

'Miss Celia wants tea,' Laura said rinsing the jug and glass under the tap. 'But you seem to have your hands full already.'

Mrs Fraser snorted ungraciously. 'A drinks party— and at the last moment—expecting cheese straws and canapés to appear from thin air.'

'I'm sorry.' Laura walked warily. 'Is there anything I can do to help?'

'I can cope, thank you.' The older woman's voice was ungracious but Laura was used to that. 'Although——' she paused. 'Well, you could get a tea tray ready, and save me the job.'

Laura's heart sank. She'd hoped to deliver the message and escape upstairs to her room. But being allowed to make any contribution was a concession, she thought drily. She'd never been the housekeeper's favourite as a child, but since her return, the woman's attitude had been practically hostile.

So, she filled the kettle and set it to boil, while she laid a tray with cups and saucers under Mrs Fraser's critical eye.

'You could have knocked me down with a feather when I saw who was at the door,' the housekeeper volunteered at last, producing a tin of homemade biscuits from a cupboard and handing them to Laura. 'Looks more affluent than he did in the old days,' she added, with another snort. 'Back for good, is he?'

Laura shrugged. 'I really couldn't say. I understand he's here on business.'

'Not looking for a reconciliation then?' Mrs Fraser's sharp eyes were bright with malice, and Laura bit her lip, controlling a number of heated replies.

She said, with cool politeness. 'As I said, Mrs Fraser, he seems to have business in the area. Would you like me to take the tray in as well.'

The housekeeper sniffed, and turned back to her baking. 'If it wouldn't trouble you too much.'

'Oh, you've only brought two cups,' Celia exclaimed as Laura set the tray down on the low table which fronted the sofa. 'But I meant you to join us sweetie, naturally.'

'Thank you,' Laura said evenly. 'But I have things to do.'

'Nothing that can't wait, I'm sure.' Celia gave her a limpid look. 'You're being rather silly, you know. We're bound to be seeing a lot of Jason once the Tristan projects get under way locally. You may as well get accustomed to the fact, and have tea with us in a civilised manner.'

'Civilised' was fast becoming her least favourite word, Laura reflected bitterly. She said tautly, 'Some other time.'

'There's no time like the present,' Jason said smoothly. He rose to his feet, his lean body straightening in one lithe movement. 'Sit down, Laura. I'm sure your cousin won't mind fetching another cup.'

To judge by the expression which fleetingly crossed Celia's face, he'd made a big mistake there, Laura thought drily.

She began, 'I'll get it . . .' but his hands descended on her shoulders, pushing her firmly down on to the softness of the sofa.

'I said sit down,' he reminded her gently.

Celia said with a small, artificial laugh. 'How very masterful. I'd better go and get that cup.'

The door closed behind her. Laura sat rigidly, her hands linked round her knees in a parody of relaxation, staring down at the carpet.

'Alone together over the teacups,' Jason said softly. 'What a moment of pure nostalgia for us to savour, darling.'

She said, 'What the hell are you doing here, Jason? Whatever impression Celia may have given, you must know you're not welcome in this house.'

'On the contrary,' he sounded amused. 'I confidently expect to become the year's most honoured guest. As for why I'm here—I came to return this to you.' He took a small gold cylinder from his pocket, and tossed it towards her. 'So, if you were imagining that I'd followed you here, drooling with lust, think again.'

She looked stupidly down at her own lipstick. 'Where

...? Oh, it must have fallen out of my bag when I dropped it.'

'Right,' he said unemotionally. 'And I assumed you might need it at some time.'

'It could have waited,' she said. 'You could have given it to Fergie—my uncle's secretary. Anyway, thank you.'

'Graciously spoken,' Jason approved sardonically. He sat down at the other end of the sofa, leaning back, very much at his ease. 'Well, aren't you going to pour the tea?'

She shrugged. 'I'm sure Celia would prefer to do that. She's the hostess here, after all.'

'And you're what? The skivvy? The Cinderella of the establishment, with that lipstick the nineteen eighties equivalent of the glass slipper?'

She bit her lip. 'Please don't be ridiculous. And don't—don't judge by appearances either. I'm glad to do anything I can for Uncle Martin. It's the least I can offer in exchange for a roof over my head.'

'You had a roof over your head,' he said softly. 'A perfectly adequate one—although not admittedly as flash as this.' He looked around, his lips curling slightly. 'What charming decor? Your choice?'

He knew perfectly well that it wasn't, she thought stormily. On one of their few visits to his house during their brief marriage, she'd told him how much she loved the quiet charm of this room, with the pale silk wallpaper and faded chintzes which had furnished it then.

She said quietly, 'It was time for a change.'

'A telling phrase,' he said cynically, and the colour ran into her face. She leaned forward and began to pour the tea, praying that her hand wouldn't shake and betray her. 'And not the only change,' he added. 'There's also yourself. You've allowed yourself to become a shadow, instead of the flesh and blood I remember. If I painted you now, what would there be—just a soft blur in the background?'

'You still paint?' To her annoyance, the question was out before she could prevent it.

'Sometimes.' He sent her a cool smile as he took the cup from her. 'If I can find a subject which appeals to me. I have to be more selective these days, now that my time is limited.'

Underneath her confusion of anger and anxiety, she was conscious of the stirrings of regret. He'd been a truly talented painter, and his work had just started to sell, even though he'd refused to compromise his arresting, almost violent style. He'd believed in himself, and in his work, and it seemed impossible that now he'd relegated it to the role of a hobby, to be pursued in whatever leisure he allowed himself.

As if he could read her thoughts, he said, 'It was time for a change,' mocking her with her own words.

She drew a breath. 'And—the change was Tristan Construction? How did that come about?'

'Through the death of my father,' he said expressionlessly. 'The company belonged to him.'

She swallowed. 'I—I didn't know. I'm sorry.'

'Are you, Laura? I can't imagine why. You never knew him. In fact, you didn't even believe he existed.' She was suddenly and chillingly aware of the anger in him, the violence just below the surface.

She said tightly, 'I had good reason—if you remember.'

'Yes, I remember,' he said too gently. 'Every detail of the whole bloody mess is indelibly engraved on my memory, darling, believe me.'

'You both look very fierce,' Celia said from the doorway. 'Would you rather throw this cup than drink out of it?'

Laura said levelly, 'I'd really prefer to do neither. So, if you'll both excuse me.'

She got up, and he watched her, his mouth smiling, but his eyes grim. He said, 'Until later then.'

'Later,' she repeated.

'The drinks party, sweetie,' Celia chirped. 'For the Tristan executives. I've decided to do my bit for Caswells at last. Aren't you pleased?'

'Over the moon,' Laura said wildly, wondering why Celia hadn't been strangled at birth.

Celia pouted prettily. 'Laura's always telling me I don't take sufficient interest in the company. But all that's going to change from now on.' She sent him a mischievously provocative look from under her lashes. 'In fact, I'm going to take the most amazing interest in every aspect of its dealings.' She giggled. 'This party is only the start.'

Jason smiled at her. 'It should be a truly memorable evening for us all,' he said.

His tone was light, but over Celia's blonde head, he looked at Laura, and his eyes were bleak with a warning it was impossible to ignore.

She walked to the door, and left them alone together.

CHAPTER THREE

SHE found she was still clutching the lipstick. She unclenched her hand, and put the little tube down on the dressing table in her room. It had left marks on her hand where she'd been gripping it, and she touched them almost wonderingly.

She sank down on the stool, and stared at her pale reflection in the mirror. It was true, she thought. She was like a shadow—like the moon to Celia's golden, confident sun. It had been the same all their lives—even at school. Celia had been 'the pretty one' and she'd been 'the quiet one' which she supposed was a kind way of saying 'the plain one'.

She supposed her parents had thought her beautiful. But since then—only one other person . . .

She bit into the softness of her lower lip, relishing the pain, if only it would help to quell the deeper pain inside her.

All this time, she thought, she'd been struggling to put her life back together again, to reconcile herself to the fact that Jason would never be part of it again. All this time—and, it seemed—all for nothing.

Divorce was like surgery, she thought wearily. And while the operation had been a complete success, the patient, apparently, had not recovered.

She gave a swift shiver, and stood up determinedly. What a triumph for Jason if he could only know how completely she'd been thrown by his sudden reappearance and its implications. But he must never know, she told herself. He'd said their paths were bound to cross, but that was not necessarily so. They could operate on parallel lines, and never meet.

In the meantime, she could get out of this drinks party Celia had arranged, by 'phoning Alan and asking if they could meet in Burngate. He would be disappointed, she supposed, as she went over to her wardrobe and scanned along the hanging rail for something to wear, but under the circumstances that couldn't be helped.

None of the garments hanging there were particularly spectacular, she thought with a little mental shrug. They were what Celia disparagingly called 'background clothes', neutral in colour and design—part of her recovery camouflage. Yet now she was conscious of a vague dissatisfaction as she selected a silky grey crêpe, with full sleeves and a deeply slashed crossover bodice, and draped it across a chair while she went into her tiny adjoining bathroom to shower and wash her hair.

Usually, she blow-dried her hair, then used a hot brush to curve the ends underneath, and around her face, but as she hadn't managed the trim she needed, she decided she would wear her hair up for a change.

She was experimenting, twisting the silky strands into various styles, when she heard sounds of departure from downstairs, and a car engine starting up in the drive.

She rose, and trod barefoot across the carpet to her window and looked out from the shelter of the curtain. Inevitably, he was driving the Jaguar which had occupied her space in the car park. If she'd decided to park in the drive, instead of taking the car round to the garages at the back, she would have seen it, recognised it—maybe even been warned.

She watched him drive away towards the town, then turned back to her dressing table with a little sigh. He would be back.

It occurred to her that she ought to warn Mrs Fraser that she wouldn't be there for dinner. She didn't want to add a charge of thoughtlessness to the crime sheet against her. And she could 'phone Alan at the same time.

The first errand was simple enough, but the second was more tricky. The 'phone rang and rang, but there was no answer. She groaned silently as she replaced the receiver. She would have to try later.

When she got back to her room, Celia was stretched on the bed waiting for her. She was smiling, her eyes sparkling with a mixture of amusement and malice.

'Well, sweetie, you're quite a dark horse aren't you— but rather silly to think you could ever keep such a delectable man all to yourself. It was just as well I was still in Switzerland while it was all going on, or I might have tried to steal him myself. And he wouldn't have got away from me so easily.' She gave a little laugh. 'He could hardly believe we were cousins.'

Laura picked up her comb again, forcing suddenly nerveless fingers back to their former task. She said tonelessly, 'Well, he wouldn't be the first to find it amazing that we're related.'

'That's true,' Celia agreed limpidly. 'But he's by far the most interesting to date.' She stretched like a little cat. 'Poor Laura. It was being rather optimistic, sweetie, to think you could ever hold his interest for long.'

Laura's fingers gripped the edge of the dressing table. She was used to Celia, she thought, inured to the kind of jibes she excelled at, but for the first time she was tempted to rake her nails down that lovely, contemptuous face.

She said with no particular expression, 'Well, I didn't labour under that particular misapprehension for very long.'

Celia giggled. 'No, indeed. It can't be many men who are unfaithful to their wives during the first year of marriage. Your little honeymoon didn't last long at all.' She paused, her eyes fixed almost avidly on Laura's mirrored reflection. 'And did you really not know about the Tristan Construction connection? Don't you think the whole thing's quite fascinating?'

Laura shrugged, carelessly she hoped. 'It's hardly any of my concern. We're divorced—remember?'

'How could I forget?' Celia sounded gloating. 'And I'm glad you had the sense to let him go without a struggle, Laura. It's never very dignified fighting a battle you simply aren't capable of winning.'

Laura dug a last hairpin viciously into the top-knot she'd created, almost transfixing her scalp in the process. 'Frankly, I don't think that aspect ever occurred to me.' She was surprised to realise this was the truth. She'd been too hurt, too shattered by Jason's infidelity to want to do anything but crawl away and lick the wounds he'd inflicted. To somehow learn to endure the blow she'd suffered to her new-found, fragile confidence in her womanhood.

'It would have occurred to me,' Celia said complacently. 'And I think—yes, I really do think I'd have fought tooth and nail—and won. But that's the difference between us, isn't it, sweetie?'

'One of them, certainly,' Laura returned. Dissatisfied, she pulled the pins out of her tawny hair and let it spill round her face again.

'So, I can take it you won't start fighting now?' Celia lifted a hand and studied its perfectly manicured nails.

'I don't think I understand.' Laura picked up her jar of moisturiser and began to apply it sparingly to her face and throat.

'Then think.' Celia's voice sounded almost strident suddenly. 'He doesn't belong to you anymore, as you've just admitted. In fact it's a moot point whether he ever actually belonged to you at all, even if you did wangle a wedding ring out of him. So, I take it you'll have no real objection if I have him instead now?'

Laura's mouth felt so dry, she felt as if her lips might crack open and bleed as she forced the words between them. 'No, I've no reason, and certainly no right to object, but I should warn you your father may well feel very differently. He never liked Jason or approved of him, and I don't think he'll care for the fact that you've invited him here this evening.'

Celia smiled. 'He may not have liked the penniless artist who married his little niece for her money, then— done her wrong, as the saying is. But the Jason Wingard who's now the managing director of a big, successful firm like Tristan Construction is a very different proposition. He's no fortune hunter now to be shown the door, but an extremely eligible, and incredibly sexy man.'

'Perhaps.' Laura could hardly believe how calm she sounded, how collected, when emotionally she felt ravaged. 'But I still doubt if your father will see it like that, no matter how rich Jason may be now.'

'If you think for one moment that Daddy would let any personal feelings stand in the way of business, then you don't know him,' Celia told her coolly. 'You told me yourself how important this contract is, and like a dutiful daughter I intend to spare no effort to make sure that Caswells gets this contract, along with any other goodies Tristan Construction might care to throw our way. Your ex-husband was telling me, when you so thoughtlessly interrupted us, that they're heavily committed to private housing over the next few years, as well as the local projects. And housing estates mean show houses—completely furnished, including carpets.'

'You seem to have it all worked out,' Laura said.

'I have.' Celia lifted herself off the bed, straightening a crease from her shirt. 'I just want to make sure, Laura darling, that you aren't going to be the skeleton at any little feasts I may plan.' She laughed. 'Because I intend to mix the firm's business with a hell of a lot of pleasure.'

'So, why tell me?' Laura began to apply foundation

in quick jerky movements. 'What do you want from me? Surely not my blessing?'

'Hardly.' Celia's eyes, bright and predatory, met hers. 'No, this is just a timely reminder that Jason is no longer your affair, and that I don't intend to brook any interference from you or anyone else. You had him, and you couldn't hold him. Well, that's tough, but it's the way the cookie crumbles sometimes. Now, it's my turn.'

Laura replaced the lid on the little jar. She said slowly, 'Celia—Jason may be legally single, but that doesn't mean that he's necessarily—free. Doesn't it disturb you that there may still be other—priorities in his life?'

'Why should it?' Celia gave a negligent shrug. 'I'm not a naïve, narrow-minded little schoolgirl. And I'll make damned sure his sole priority in future is me.'

'Then I wish you luck.' Laura rose too. 'Now I'd be glad of some privacy. I'd like to get dressed.'

Celia's eyes swept her cousin's slim figure, wrapped in its cotton robe, and her lip curled. She said, 'What a ridiculous prude you are, Laura. It's little wonder Jason found himself another woman.'

As the door closed behind her, Laura dropped limply back on to her dressing stool. Celia's behaviour was incredible, even by her own standards, plumbing new depths of selfishness and arrogance.

But then, there was little wonder, she thought ruefully. Following the death of his wife, Martin Caswell had poured his energy and considerable resources into making sure his only daughter had everything she wanted in life, almost before the wish had been expressed. It wasn't a healthy situation, and Celia had grown up believing that the world was hers for the taking.

And generally, the world went along with Celia's belief, Laura was forced to admit. Her name had been linked, at one time or another, with all the wealthiest young men in the locality, but never very seriously, or for very long.

But now Celia had seen a man she wanted at last, and she intended to go after him with that incredible single-mindedness which had always characterised her devotion to her own interests.

And she really thinks, Laura thought with growing anger, that I'm going to sit back and watch her.

She slipped off her robe and began to dress, struggling with normally simple hooks and fasteners.

For the past three years, she'd looked on this house as a refuge, and ignored Celia's vagaries out of gratitude to Uncle Martin. But in view of Celia's expressed intentions, this could not go on.

She thought, 'I've got to get out of here, and soon.'

There was a rap on the door, and she jumped nervously, laddering the tights she was smoothing on to her slender legs.

Mrs Fraser appeared. 'Mr Caswell has come home, and is asking for you,' she announced magisterially. 'He's in the study, and he doesn't seem best pleased, so I wouldn't keep him waiting.'

When Laura entered the study a little while later, she decided the housekeeper had not exaggerated her uncle's peevishness. His usually ruddy colour had deepened alarmingly, and his mouth was set in sour lines.

'This is a damned mess,' he greeted Laura fretfully, his tone faintly accusing, as if in some way it was all her fault. 'Had you any idea this was likely to happen?'

Laura sighed. 'Uncle Martin, you know quite well I haven't seen or heard from Jason since before the divorce. The only communication we had after I left was through our solicitors.'

'Yes, yes, I suppose so.' He drummed his fingers on the desk, frowning heavily. He said half to himself. 'And I thought we were rid of him.' He gave a short laugh. 'Well, it seems we must make the best of it. There's no room for personalities in business, after all. What's past is past, and the Tristan contract could be a lifesaver for us. So I hope I can depend on you, Laura, not to make waves.'

Laura's hands clenched together. 'Behave in a civilised manner, do you mean?' she enquired ironically. 'Now, where have I heard that before?'

Her uncle shrugged irritably. 'What the hell does it matter? And it's exactly what I mean. We can't let our personal feelings get in the way, Laura. Our first loyalty has to be to the firm.' He paused. 'Even Celia is going to make every effort . . .'

'So I understand.' Laura looked at him drily. 'Starting off with a cocktail party this very evening. How will you feel, entertaining Jason under this roof again?'

'I'll do what I need to do.' Martin Caswell walked over to the tray of decanters situated on a side table and poured himself a generous measure of whisky. 'And so will you, my child, if you know what's good for you.'

'I see.' Laura ran the tip of her tongue over her dry lips. 'Uncle Martin—don't you think it might be better if I went right away from here? This is a very embarrassing situation for all of us and . . .'

'Nonsense.' Martin Caswell slammed his glass down on the desk, slopping some of the contents on to the polished surface. 'Good God, girl, divorce is no novelty these days. You're not unique. Besides where would you go? What could you do?'

She looked at him. 'I'm a good cook. I can keep house. Even these days there are jobs . . .'

'You already have a job—here.' He glared at her. 'My God, Laura, I thought you had some gratitude in you. I take you in when you're on your knees, and just when I most need your help, your support, you threaten to walk out.'

'Am I supposed to have no feelings at all?' she asked hoarsely.

'Feelings? Don't talk to me about feelings when the whole future of Caswells could be at stake.' He threw himself back in his chair. 'They want to use the new Fibrona in both these projects they're committed to locally. If they do, and they like it, it could be worth a fortune in advertising for us. My God, Laura, the stuff isn't even properly in production yet—the lab still want to do more tests on the fireproofing element—yet somehow Tristan Construction have heard about it, and they've beaten a path to our door. I've always said Fibrona was revolutionary, and this proves it. It will the saving of Caswells, I tell you.'

Laura said urgently, 'But it isn't the only fibre we produce—and we have other customers besides Tristans. Aren't we putting all our eggs into one rather chancy basket? Supposing we invest heavily in the production of Fibrona, and then Tristan Construction decide they don't want it after all. What then?'

'Of course they want it,' he said. 'Why else would they have come to us?'

He made it sound unanswerable, but Laura had an uneasy feeling that it was not.

She said quietly, 'Uncle Martin—I only wish I knew,' and left the room, closing the door quietly behind her.

From the windowseat in her room, she watched the cars begin to arrive for the party. She had no choice. She'd rung Alan's cottage twice in the intervening period, but had received no answer. So—she would wait up here until she saw his car, and persuade him to slip away quietly, without getting involved.

She'd done a lot of hard thinking while she was waiting, but none of the conclusions she'd reached were very happy ones. Uncle Martin was a worried man, and had been for sometime, and like other worried men he was prone to clutch at straws. But that didn't mean that Jason had walked back into their lives with a lifeline.

He, she thought soberly, had no reason to love Caswells, or wish to do them any favours.

She had tried many times to blot out of her mind the agonising bitterness of that last scene between them. No-one should pay too much credence to things said or done in savage anger, she told herself. But that didn't alter the fact that one of the last things Jason had said to her was that he would make Martin Caswell pay for his role in the breach between them.

She tried to reassure herself that it had simply been said in the heat of the moment. Tried to tell herself that however cynically immoral his behaviour, Jason was not a vengeful man.

Or was he? What did she know of him, after all? What had she ever known? she asked herself despairingly.

In the early days of their relationship, she'd probed, trying to establish details about his childhood, upbringing, education, family—all the things which had contributed to make the man she'd fallen in love with. But he'd always blocked her questions abruptly, telling her the past didn't matter—that it was only the present and the future which counted.

In fact, she'd assumed he had no family—that his reluctance to discuss his former life stemmed from the fact that he'd been brought up in a children's home, or similar institution.

The discovery that his parents were both living had only been the first of the shocks which had torn their married life apart.

And now, he was back and in a position of power. A position where he could hurt Caswell as easily as he could extend a helping hand.

It would be fatally easy for him to encourage her uncle's company to rush Fibrona into production, then back out at the last moment. Easy—and potential financial devastation for Caswells.

If he wanted revenge for the humiliation that the discovery of his double life, and the subsequent divorce must have caused him, then the weapons for that revenge were at his fingertips. He was a man who kept his secrets well, she thought bitterly. This time, his motives and intentions would all be locked in his mind, safe from any form of investigation.

All she had to go on was a gut reaction that nothing was as simple as it seemed. And Uncle Martin was a hard-headed man. Did he really suspect nothing? Whatever miracle qualities the chemists might claim for Fibrona, she couldn't believe they were sufficient to have brought Jason Wingard back into their lives.

And she was no longer naïve enough to think it could just be coincidence either.

People were arriving all the time. Celia had been busy. She seemed to have invited half the neighbourhood as well as the members of the Caswell board, and the Tristan executives.

She could hear the faint hum of voices from downstairs each time the drawing room door opened, and Celia's laugh floating above them all, as sparkling as springwater.

Laura had watched her go downstairs. Celia had looked dazzling, all the stops pulled out, in a dress of midnight blue taffeta, with a huge stiffened collar framing and accentuating her blonde hair.

She tried to tell herself that for once Jason might have met his match in Celia, but she didn't believe it in her heart. Whether or not Celia deserved it, she felt anxious for her.

She'd even considered seeking Jason out—not here, but at whatever hotel he was staying at and telling him bluntly that she didn't believe he wanted to bury the past.

She wanted to say, 'Whatever residue of bitterness remains, let it stay just between the two of us. If you must punish someone for what happened, then punish me, not my family. My uncle only acted as he did to protect me, because he loved me.'

She tried to imagine his reaction to her words. Tried, and failed.

It was a relief to see Alan's red Mini backing carefully into a space between two far more opulent vehicles. She snatched up her bag and wrap and flew downstairs just as the doorbell sounded, calling, 'I'll get it,' to Mrs Fraser.

Alan was smiling broadly as she opened the door. He handed her a cellophane box. 'Happy restaurant opening.'

The box contained flowers—freesias tied with a bow of silver ribbon.

She heard herself say, 'How lovely. No-one's ever brought me flowers before.'

Except once, her memory reminded her relentlessly, and they were freesias too. Bought from a street stall on your wedding day as you walked together to the registrar's.

She said, 'I'll put them in water.'

Alan looked surprised. 'You're supposed to wear them, I think.'

'But if you do, they die almost at once, and it's such a shame.' She put the box down gently. 'Do you mind if we leave at once—have our drink in a pub after all? My cousin's having a cocktail party—business and very boring. I don't really want us to be caught up in it.'

He was disappointed, she could see that at once. It was the first time he'd been to the house, and he'd obviously been looking forward to seeing more of it than just the hall.

She was going to say something reassuring about

other times, when the drawing room door opened, and Celia said, 'Another guest? How lovely. Do come in.'

Laura froze. Behind Celia, towering head and shoulders above her was Jason. He was smiling, but his eyes as they met Laura's were as bleak as winter. Returning to this house had clearly revived memories for him too, and she knew that Uncle Martin was fooling himself if he thought the past could simply be brushed aside where this man was concerned. That hard look told her more openly than words that Jason had neither forgiven nor forgotten anything.

She said sharply, 'Actually, we're just going out.'

'Rubbish.' Celia walked across the hall, smiling and holding out her hand. 'I presume you must be Alan. Laura's told me such a lot about you, and it's nice to meet you at last. But you surely don't intend to run away without having just one little drink.' She linked her arm through his, her smile widening. 'I've had to speak to Cousin Laura before about keeping all the really attractive men to herself.'

'Well—a whisky and soda would be marvellous,' Alan accepted, trying not to sound too eager, and failing.

Laura's heart sank as she followed them into the drawing room. It was something of a relief to find that the party was on the point of breaking up. People had their last drinks in their hands, and some were beginning to edge discreetly towards the door.

Alan had his drink, and was blossoming rapidly, as Celia led him round the room introducing him to people. Laura, holding a dry sherry she didn't want, had no desire to follow round the room in their wake, so she stayed beside the french windows, watching the evening sun dappling through the trees on to the smooth lawn.

She could hear her uncle's laugh booming out. He enjoyed socialising, playing the expansive host, and she'd always found this rather endearing. Now she was disconcerted and alarmed to find how readily he'd adapted to this intolerable situation which had been forced on them.

If he was determined to look on Tristan Construction as a potential saviour, Laura doubted whether he would give the slightest credence to any further warnings she might proffer. She would probably be accused of prejudice, she thought wryly.

'You look anxious,' Jason said, and she jumped violently. She'd been so lost in thought, she'd been totally unaware of his approach across the room.

'Let me take that before you spill it.' He removed the untouched glass from her hand and put it down on one of the litter of small tables used on these occasions. His hand brushed one of the floating sleeves of her dress. 'What's this intended to be—a cloak of invisibility?'

'If so, it clearly hasn't worked,' she said coolly, resisting an impulse to wrench the fragile material out of his hand. 'And I'm sure there are more important people in the room for you to talk to than myself.'

'At the moment, I can't think of one.' He spoke softly, but she was aware of the glint of anger in his eyes. 'You're very anxious to be rid of me.'

'Under the circumstances that's hardly surprising,' she retorted.

'But not very flattering. I don't think your beautiful cousin would be pleased at your sabotaging her goodwill campaign. She's clearly gone to a great deal of trouble,' he added, glancing round the room. 'Caswells must be in a deeper mess than I suspected.'

Laura bit her lip. 'I don't think there's anything very special about this party,' she disclaimed.

'So Caswells push the boat out like this for all their potential customers?' His brows lifted sceptically. 'How very extravagant. I hope they don't expect us to reciprocate. I don't think the resources of the Swan Hotel could cope.'

She said expressionlessly, 'I don't suppose that's the intention at all.'

He looked at her, his mouth slanting mockingly. 'I'm sure there's a world of hidden meaning behind that innocent remark, but I'm not going to pursue it—at the moment anyway. I think it would be safer if I just introduce you to some people instead.'

'That's not necessary,' Laura said, more sharply than she intended. 'I—I mean—I have a dinner date. We'll be leaving at any moment.'

'I don't think so,' he said smoothly. 'Your—er—date is well into his second drink, and having a whale of a time. I hope they'll hold the table for you wherever you're going.' He put a hand under her elbow. 'Now come and meet Robert Leng and the others.'

She hung back, staring up at him with hostile eyes. 'Just how do you intend to introduce me—as your ex-wife? I presume they all know you're divorced.'

'Robert does.' His eyes narrowed as he looked down at her. 'I don't know about the others, and it doesn't really concern me.'

'Another of your little secrets, in other words,' she said bitterly. 'How is it that you actually took this Robert Leng into your confidence?'

'He's an old friend,' he said harshly. 'And he was my father's deputy for many years.'

'Until you walked in and took over?' Laura raised her eyebrows. 'That must have been a strain on the friendship, surely. And how did your board react to having a complete amateur in the seat of power? Or are you just a figurehead?'

'On the contrary,' he said too-pleasantly. 'I happen to be a qualified architect.'

'Another little detail you forgot to mention.' Her breasts rose and fell as she drew a deep, stormy breath.

'So—what was the painting? Just a temporary aberration?'

'If you like,' he drawled. 'You sound aggrieved, Laura. Should I have told you I was the heir to Tristan Construction after all? Would it have made you readier to turn a blind eye to my—marital failings perhaps?'

There was a loaded pause, then she said huskily, 'That's a swinish thing to say. There were no circumstances—none—under which I would have stayed married to you, and you know it.'

'Of course not,' he said softly. 'I was the mercenary one, of course, the one with an eye to the main chance. I'd almost forgotten that.'

'I thought you remembered everything.' She was beginning to tremble again, her fingers curling defensively into her palms.

'I suspect that, like you, my sweet ex-wife, I have a selective memory.' He gave a slight shrug. 'If you only want to recall what a bastard I was—that's your prerogative. But I'm entitled to my own reminiscences—and they're rather different. For instance, I remember how inhibited you were in bed, just at first, and how passionate you soon became. I remember how you used to wake me by biting my shoulder when you wanted to make love.' His swift grin taunted her unbearably. 'In fact I used to pretend to be asleep because it was so fantastic to feel you moving against me, wanting me.'

Bright spots of colour burned in her face. She had to fight to hang on to her control. She said coolly, 'I was a naïve child, Jason. Of course you could turn me on. But if I'd been older and wiser, I'd have probably realised that a superb lover was all you were—that you failed every other requirement as a husband.'

Just for a moment, something flickered in his face, but he said lightly enough, 'Better luck next time, darling. I hope you have something better in mind than the current boyfriend.'

She glared at him. 'You know nothing about him,' she began.

'Except that he's a loser,' he came back at her remorselessly. 'I don't need to know anything else. Nor should you.'

From behind him, Celia exclaimed, 'So there you are, hiding in this corner. I must say you both look very serious,' she added with a giggle, but the look she shot Laura was far from amiable.

Jason turned towards her, shrugging lightly, his gaze skimming smilingly over the charming picture she presented. 'Just talking over old times,' he said. 'That can be a serious business.'

Celia pouted charmingly, sliding her arm proprietorially through his. 'I'll have to take your word for that.'

Laura moved towards Alan, who had followed Celia over. 'Isn't it time we were going?' she suggested quietly.

'Going where?' Celia had ears like radar screens on occasion.

'I'm attending the opening of a new restaurant in town, and I'm taking Laura as my guest.' Alan sounded pompous suddenly.

'How absolutely super.' Celia's eyes widened ingenuously. 'Are you only allowed to take one guest? I've never actually been to a restaurant opening.'

She made it sound as if a lifetime ambition had been thwarted, Laura thought wearily.

She said, 'As a matter of fact, it's part of Alan's job—not just a joyride.'

'Oh, but it would be such fun.' Celia smiled appealingly at Alan. 'Jason, darling, don't you agree?'

He looked faintly amused. 'You can't freeload on someone else's party, my child. If you want to be taken to dinner, we can eat at the hotel.'

'But we could pay for our meal, couldn't we, Alan?

And whatever the food is like, it has to be better than the Swan Hotel. Tinned soup, and frozen vegetables,' she added with an artistic shiver.

Laura's lips tightened. Celia was no gourmet. She was quoting a recent column of Alan's in *The Echo*, which had criticised the standard of cooking in both the town's hotels, and Alan was looking suitably gratified.

'Of course it would be all right,' he said largely. 'My invitation doesn't specify any actual number, and it's publicity they want, after all, so the more the merrier. I'll say you're with me.'

'Which will make everything quite all right,' Jason murmured sardonically.

Laura flinched inwardly, but Alan was totally oblivious, visibly swelling with pleasure and importance.

The evening was steadily becoming more horrendous, she thought, wondering if she could invent a last minute headache—a fainting spell—a tumour on the brain.

'Then it's all settled,' Celia said gaily. 'I do love surprises, don't you?'

It wasn't clear whether she was addressing anyone in particular and no-one answered.

No, Laura thought, as Alan helped her on with her wrap. I don't like surprises, and today I've had more than enough already.

It was small consolation to know that Jason probably disliked this new turn of events just as much as she did.

She thought, 'But it's only for this evening. Just for one evening. If I can get through this, I need never see him again.'

And found, with shock, that was no real consolation either.

CHAPTER FOUR

THEY'D travelled about half a mile, when Alan said, 'You're very quiet.'

As she hadn't uttered a word since they left the house, this was hardly very perceptive, but Laura resisted the impulse to snap as much back at him.

He went on rather anxiously, 'I hope you didn't mind my inviting your cousin and her friend to this opening with us. It was just—well, he seems pretty much of a man of the world, and if the restaurant is any good, he could spread the word among his company executives. After all, Tristan Construction are going to be moving in very soon now—practically taking over, in fact.'

Laura winced. 'Will the town ever survive it?' she asked rather ironically.

Alan looked surprised. 'But it's a marvellous thing for everyone. More building, increased trade—benefits all round.'

She shrugged, 'Then that's all that needs to be said.' Her voice sounded high, and just a little strident, and he gave her an uneasy sideways glance. He could see the evening going wrong before his eyes, she thought with swift compunction, and tried to make amends. 'I'm sorry—I'm just a little uptight. It's been quite a day, one way and another. But I'm sure it's going to be a lovely evening,' she added gently. 'What's this restaurant called?'

'The Petronelle.' On sure ground again, Alan launched eagerly into a resumé of what details he knew about it, and this safely occupied the remainder of the journey.

The Petronelle was already half-full when they arrived, and a photographer from *The Echo* was moving among the tables, taking pictures.

Laura looked around her, feigning an interest in the decor to avoid Jason's cynical gaze, but in spite of herself, she found her interest being caught. Someone had obviously worked very hard, complementing the soft glow of the panelled walls with lots of greenery, and good quality pastel table linen. If the food was as good, she thought critically, then the Petronelle should be a success.

Her eyes widened as she saw the girl in the Liberty print dress who was advancing to welcome them, and show them to their table.

Regardless of the fact that Alan was in the middle of introducing himself as *The Echo* correspondent, she said, 'Bethany? Is it really you?'

The girl swung round, her brows lifting, a delighted grin spreading across her face. 'Laura Caswell, by all that's wonderful. How on earth do you come to be here?'

'Actually, she came with me,' Alan said a mite huffily.

Bethany turned back to him at once. 'Then please accept my undying gratitude. We were at cookery school together, and then for no good reason, we lost touch. What in the world happened to you, Laura? You got your diploma and—vanished.'

'It's a long story.' Laura was uneasily aware of Jason, standing close behind her. 'But what about you? You were planning to find a millionaire with a yacht and feed him cholesterol as you cruised the Bahamas. Burngate is a long way from Nassau.'

'Don't I know it? I started work in a London hotel on my way to the docks, and ended by marrying the chef.' Bethany's smile held tenderness. 'He's in the kitchen at this moment, praying. We have a lot riding on the success of this place.' She took Laura's hands and squeezed them. 'This evening's going to be hell, and I'm going to be run off my feet, or at least I hope so, but promise me you won't vanish again. For one thing, I want you to meet Mike.' She signalled to one of the mobcapped waitresses. 'Champagne, Jenny, please.'

'Well, well,' Celia said as they took their seats. 'This seems to be your day for being reunited with old friends, doesn't it sweetie?' Her tone dripped honey.

Alan said rather disagreeably, 'So this place belongs to friends of yours. She seems very young to be running her own business.'

Laura said calmly, 'But I can promise she's had a training in catering second to none. Bethany did the whole course, not the year's diploma which I took. Anyway, why don't we have our meal before we start passing judgment?'

Alan flushed slightly as he picked up his menu, and Laura sighed inwardly as she studied hers. It wasn't his fault that the evening wasn't going as he expected. She had no appetite at all, but for Bethany's sake she had to make an effort, so she chose melon, followed by a dish of chicken breasts cooked in cream and white wine. Jason chose beef in burgundy, and Celia opted for Sole Veronique after some pretty dithering, and appeals to everyone else to help her make up her mind. Alan, rather to Laura's amusement, chose all the most difficult dishes on the menu.

Look, she wanted to say to him, you're doing a piece for the local paper, not a test meal for the Good Food Guide.

They drank the new restaurant's health in champagne, and then Alan agonised over the wine list to an extent which Laura found embarrassing. He was obviously out to establish himself as a connoisseur in Celia and

Jason's eyes, she realised ruefully, and was failing
miserably. She saw her cousin send Jason a covert
glance of contemptuous amusement, and cringed
inwardly.

But the food, when it came, was perfectly cooked and
expertly presented, and the wines Alan had so
ponderously chosen complemented it well, she had to
admit, wishing at the same time that he was drinking
less of it himself. His comments on his food were
appreciative but over-loud, and he was making
ostentatious notes on the corner of his menu. She began
to wonder uneasily just how much whisky he'd
consumed at the cocktail party. Her uncle, she knew,
tended to pour with a lavish hand, and had taught Celia
to do the same.

She hoped he would refuse the inevitable cognacs
they were offered with their coffee, and was frankly
dismayed when he accepted not just the first offer, but
the second, especially when she saw the swift glance
Jason sent him, and the faint mordant twist of his
mouth.

All through the meal, she'd been aware of him sitting
opposite to her—conscious that he was watching her,
the grey eyes flicking restlessly from her face to her
throat and shoulders, half-revealed by the low neckline
of the smoky dress, then down to the glimpse it
afforded of the shadowy cleft between her breasts. She
was as physically aware of him, as if he'd been touching
her with his hands instead of his eyes. She watched, as if
hypnotised, the way the lean brown fingers cupped the
brandy goblet, and knew, the breath thickening in her
throat, that he was deliberately trying to evoke other
more intimate memories.

For Jason, lovemaking had been yet another art form
to be explored, Laura thought with an uncomfortable
twist of the heart. He'd been so unhurried with her at
first, so patient with her initial shyness, knowing, she

supposed bitterly, remembering his earlier taunt, that his patience would be rewarded. Eventually she'd learned to relax completely in his arms, to take as well as give, to trust him . . .

She clattered her coffee cup back into its saucer with a shaking hand. It was the betrayal of that trust she had to remember, not the warmth, the laughter, and the fierce mutual passion which had preceded it.

With something like panic, she touched Alan's arm. 'It's getting late. I think we should be going.'

'What's the hurry?' His words were slurred, she realised with irritation, aware of Celia's derisive smile. She found herself wondering again exactly how much he'd had to drink all evening.

Jason said smoothly, 'If you're tired, Laura, we can drive you home.'

'No need for that,' Alan said with a certain asperity. 'She's my guest,' he added with laboured dignity. 'And if she wants to go home—then we will.'

Laura fumbled with her wrap, hotly embarrassed. She hung back deliberately as the others made their way to the door, hoping they would be gone by the time she reached the street.

On her way out, she was waylaid by Bethany, who gave her a swift hug. 'You're invited to the post mortem tomorrow morning,' she whispered. 'Coffee about eleven. Come to the side door.'

Laura nodded, forcing a smile. 'I'll be there. And the meal was fantastic, Beth. I don't think you have a thing to worry about.'

Bethany smiled crossing her fingers, then turned to greet another departing group who also had praise to lavish. Laura was drawn into the conversation too, and it was some minutes before she could detach herself. But when she emerged from the restaurant, she found with a sinking heart that all three of them were waiting for her, Celia tapping her foot impatiently.

Laura could see at once that something was wrong. Alan was leaning against the side of his car. He was very pale suddenly, and there were beads of sweat on his face. She groaned inwardly.

Jason said grimly. 'He isn't fit to drive. The fresh air has knocked him out.'

'I have a licence. I can manage,' Laura said with a confidence she was far from feeling.

'That,' Jason said silkily, 'I doubt. Unless your diploma course included a section on dealing with drunks. And what about the terms of his car insurance—and yours, for that matter. Are you covered to drive for him, because if not the consequences could be serious if you were stopped, or had an accident?'

Laura was silent. She hadn't thought of that. At last, she said, 'There's a taxi rank in the square. We'll use that.'

'If you can persuade them to take you.' Jason shrugged powerful shoulders. 'Passengers in his condition are not exactly popular.'

She glared at him. 'Then you think of something.'

'I already have,' he said. 'I'll take you both in my car.'

Celia who had been listening petulantly to the conversation, broke in, alarmed. 'Oh, but Jason, you can't. Your lovely car—supposing he was—ill?'

He gave her a level look. 'That's a risk I'll have to take. But if the possibility upsets you, then I'll hire one of those taxis for you instead.'

Celia's face went blank, as she realised she had out-manoeuvred herself. Her voice became a little shrill. 'But why should our evening be spoiled, because Laura's—admirer can't hold his drink? It's quite ridiculous. And, after all, Laura did say she could cope . . .'

'Laura,' Jason said softly, 'is extremely capable, but I'm sure, under the circumstances, your father would wish her to have proper assistance. Particularly,' he added, 'as I suspect most of the damage was done under your roof earlier. Those were very large whiskies you were pouring for him.'

Celia shrugged delicately. 'He could have refused.'

Jason smiled down into her sulky face. 'He was so dazzled by you that he'd probably have drunk hemlock, if you'd offered it, and who can blame him?' He brushed her cheek with his hand, drawing a reluctant smile from her. 'That's better. And the evening doesn't have to end here. Laura and I will deliver the patient safely, then join you for coffee. Will that do?'

She laughed up at him. 'Mr Wingard, you think of everything. I'll have the coffee waiting.'

It was mortifying, having to wait in the street while Jason took Celia to the taxi rank. Alan was looking more ghastly with every moment that passed, and when she finally persuaded him to stop hanging on to the Mini and walk the few yards down Burngate to where Jason's Jaguar was parked, he was decidedly unsteady on his legs.

She was almost thankful when Jason reappeared round the corner from the square, covering the distance which separated them with his long, lithe stride.

'I'm sorry about this.' It almost killed her to say it.

He said shortly, 'So am I,' and that seemed to cover the subject.

It wasn't easy, persuading Alan to actually get into the Jaguar. He exhibited sudden symptoms of independence, insisting that he could drive, and wanted his own car.

'And presumably a licence to drive it with,' Jason said pleasantly. 'There's a police car not a hundred yards away. I imagine you'd be stopped before you'd got half that distance.'

Alan subsided into the passenger seat, grumbling incoherently under his breath.

Jason looked over his shoulder at Laura, sitting tensely upright on the back seat, her hands clasped in her lap. 'Wishing you'd gone with Celia?'

Yes, she thought, for all kinds of reasons . . .

She said aloud, 'Not at all. I feel rather responsible . . .'

He gave her an irritated glance, and turned on the ignition. 'Why? You didn't pour whisky down him as if it was going out of fashion, or keep filling his glass in there. He did it all by himself, and he's surely old enough now to know his own limitations and be careful.'

Laura flushed. 'Yes.'

'Yes,' he repeated with derisive emphasis. 'Now, I'm relying on you to give me directions to wherever he lives in sufficient time for me not to have to brake, or swerve, or do anything else we might live to regret. Do I make myself clear?'

She glared at him. 'As crystal,' she said bitterly.

Long before the short journey was over, Alan had fallen asleep, his head lolling and his breathing stertorous. It was a relief when they finally slid to a halt outside the cottage.

She said, 'Will he be all right?'

'He'll have a hell of a hangover tomorrow, but I think he deserves that.' Jason's voice was impatient. 'Can you bear to give me a hand with him?'

Between them, they tugged and heaved Alan out of the car. He half woke up, and started a *sotto voce* complaint about something or other, as they half-helped, half-carried him up the narrow path.

Jason looked at her. 'Key?' His brows arched interrogatively.

Laura shrugged helplessly. 'In his pockets, I suppose.' A thought struck her. 'Although he said once that he keeps a spare one under a loose tile in the porch.'

'How original,' Jason said blandly. 'I think we'll try
for that one, don't you?'

Luckily it was there. Laura retrieved it hastily, and
thrust it into the lock. The door opened, and she stood
aside while Jason took Alan into the hall.

He said, 'Where's his bedroom?'

'Upstairs, I suppose.'

'You mean you don't know?' he jibed, and she felt
the colour race into her cheeks.

Her voice shook. 'This is exactly the second time I've
been here.'

'Don't tell me you've reverted to courting in cars,
Laura.' He shook his head reprovingly. 'That's very
adolescent. And in a Mini, bloody uncomfortable.'

She was about to tell him scorchingly that she and
Alan were not courting at all, when she realised just in
time the trap she'd nearly stumbled into. Instead she
summoned a smile as cool as his own.

'How I conduct my affairs is my own business. I
don't need your advice or approval—thank God,' she
added piously.

'Don't give thanks too soon, darling, because I
haven't finished with you—not by a hell of a long
chalk.' His voice was bleak. 'Now for the sake of
argument, we'll assume the bedroom is up these stairs.
You take his feet.'

Somehow, they got him up the narrow flight and
into the room opposite the bathroom. There were
clothes strewn about, and piles of books, and a neatly
made double bed. Laura ignored the mocking glance
Jason sent her as they heaved Alan on to it, face
downwards.

She said worriedly, 'Should we—just leave him like
this?'

He sent her a bored look. 'I'll wait downstairs if you
want to undress him. But I should warn you he'll be in

no fit state to appreciate your attentions in the way they deserve.'

Laura said between her teeth, 'I didn't mean that, and you know it. But should we call a doctor or . . .?' She lifted her shoulders in a helpless little shrug.

'He's in no danger,' Jason said shortly. 'Does he make a habit of this?'

She shook her head. 'I don't think so. Certainly I've never seen him like this before. I didn't realise how much he'd had.'

'With some people, it doesn't need much. Maybe he's one of them. Anyway, he's out for the count now.' His smile was thin. 'Poor little Laura. What a disappointing end to your romantic dinner.'

'If foursomes can be said to be romantic. I'm sure Celia wouldn't agree with you.'

'She probably wouldn't,' he agreed. 'She does rather demand one's exclusive attention. I wonder if she's worth it?'

'And I'm certain you're going to find out.' Her smile was a little ragged, but it was there. 'Maybe you shouldn't keep her waiting any longer.'

'I've no intention of making her wait at all,' he said pleasantly. 'I imagine she wouldn't thank any man for a protracted wooing. She scarcely falls into the shrinking violet category.'

Unlike you. The words, unspoken, seemed to hang in the air between them.

Then Jason turned on his heel and walked out of the room, and she heard his feet on the wooden stairs.

She followed. On the second step from the bottom, her skimpy heel skidded on the narrow tread, and she fell forward with a little startled cry, her balance lost completely. His reflexes panther-sharp, he caught her, his arms closing round her, dragging her against the hard lean warmth of his body.

For a second, or perhaps for infinity, he looked down

into her anguished face, the grey eyes gleaming silver suddenly, then her mouth was possessed, plundered, ravaged by the passionate brutality of his kiss.

Her lips parted in helpless surrender. She kissed him back, exploring his mouth as demandingly as he was seeking the moist warmth of hers. His hands were pulling at the smoky dress, dragging it off her shoulders almost down to her elbows, baring her to the waist. He lifted his head and looked at her, his eyes brilliant with a fevered desire, a hectic flush staining the high cheekbones.

He said in a stranger's voice, 'All evening. Oh Christ, Laura, every second of all evening . . .' And on his lips the blasphemy sounded like a prayer.

His head bent, and his mouth took full erotic possession of what his hands had uncovered.

He was consuming her, she thought dazedly; draining the lifeblood out of her through her heated skin. A thousand little pulses all over her body were beating out the single word 'now—now—now' in an incessant, drugging rhythm.

And then she heard, with her conscious mind, the muffled sounds of movement from above which reminded her that they were not alone.

She heard Jason whisper an obscenity, and then she was free, swaying on her feet, her body languid with need, but free. His hands reached for her again, but only to drag her dress back into place. He said, 'We shouldn't be here.'

Her voice shaking, she said, 'Where can we go?'

His voice slowed to a drawl. 'Home, darling. Where else? Celia has coffee waiting for us, remember?'

The shock of it was like a knife, slicing through flesh, bone and marrow. Her whole being seemed to shrink in humiliation as she realised she has offered herself to him—and been rejected.

CHAPTER FIVE

SHE awoke some time in the night with a feeling of oppression. The bedroom seemed dark and oddly close, the air very still. Then, away in the distance she heard the sour threatening rumble of thunder and knew why she had woken.

She hated storms, especially the unexpected ones, swelling up from nowhere in the dark of a summer night. As a child, she'd always pulled the bedclothes over her head, and lain there, trembling and stifling, hoping and praying that the lightning wouldn't find her.

Too late to hope that now, she thought, staring into the blank darkness. Jason had come back into her life with all the fierceness of a summer storm, and the defensive wall she had erected round herself with such care had crumbled, showing her mercilessly how vulnerable she still was where he was concerned.

All she could do—all she had ever done—was lie still and wait for the storm to pass.

She sighed, twisting restlessly on her pillow as the sky was suddenly illuminated, and that ominous rumble deepened relentlessly. And in almost the same instant, the first sting of rain flung itself against her window.

Laura groaned and pushed the covers aside. She always slept with the casement open in summer, but she would have to close it now unless the cushions on the window seat were to be drenched.

As she knelt there, wrestling with the catch, lightning streaked across the sky again, and for a moment the houses opposite, and the garden and drive below were trapped in a glare more powerful than a searchlight, revealing the sleek lines of Jason's Jaguar, still parked near the shrubbery by the front door.

She stayed where she was, staring downwards through the streaming rivulets of rain, telling herself she was imagining things, waiting for the next betraying lightning flash.

But there was no mistake, no trick of the imagination. The car was solid fact.

She slid off the window seat and went across to the door, opening it a fraction. The whole house was still and dark. No-one but herself had been disturbed by the storm, it seemed. There were no lights on anywhere, no sound of voices to indicate that Celia still had a visitor.

She found she was gripping the door handle so tightly that her fingers were aching. Surely Celia couldn't be so indiscreet—such an utter fool . . .

She closed the door again silently, and stood, her arms wrapped protectively round her body. The answer to that was—Celia acted only as seemed best to Celia. She had never been openly promiscuous, or at least Laura had never been aware of it, if so, but she was no blushing violet either. Celia might be her junior by over a year, but it had always made Laura's head spin to think how much older in wordly wisdom her cousin had always been. By her own blithe admission, her first lover had been one of the ski instructors at her expensive and supposedly sheltered Swiss finishing school.

While I, Laura thought wryly, was still a trembling virgin.

She went quickly across the room, and got back into bed, pulling the covers around her as if the shivers running deeply through her slender body were of physical origin and could be dispelled by the comfort of a blanket. She closed her eyes, squeezing her eyelids tightly, trying to banish the images of Jason with Celia, their bodies locked together in the ageless ritual of

lovemaking. There were times when imagination could
be anguish, when memories crucified.

Only a few hours ago, she thought—only a few hours
... But if she was coldly realistic, that was probably
what it was all about. Jason had been as aroused as she
had been by those too brief, abortive moments of
passion. If Celia offered the satisfaction his body
needed, then he would take it, using her as casually and
cynically as he had always used his women.

She turned, punching her pillow into shape as the
thunder unleashed its fury overhead, and the rain
lashed at the windowpanes.

Perhaps it would have been better if she'd been able
to be like Celia, to have treated her own virginity as a
slight inconvenience to be discarded as soon as possible,
to have discreetly taken any man she fancied ever after.

In those circumstances, she and Jason would have
met, enjoyed a brief affair together and then passed on,
leaving each other virtually unscathed.

Staring into the darkness, she remembered how it had
all begun. With Julie Frant's party. She hadn't been
keen to go, but Julie had been persuasive and persistent.

'You *never* go *anywhere*,' she said plaintively. 'Come
on, Caswell, be a devil for once in your life. Stop
thinking about how to create the perfect Hollondaise
and live a little.'

Laura had given in and accepted the invitation, but
she'd regretted it almost as soon as she'd arrived at the
party, held in the large basement flat which Julie shared
with another girl. The lights were dim, the atmosphere
smoky and the music loud. Laura found herself a glass
of white wine, and retired to a corner, wondering how
soon she would be able to slip away. Julie's boyfriend
Edward was a sculptor, and taught at a local
polytechnic, and many of the guests were also involved
in the arts to a greater or lesser extent, and Laura felt
she had little in common with them, as most of them

seemed to consider that cordon bleu cooking was an unnecessary refinement in life.

'Darling.' Julie had dashed past eventually. 'If you're not dancing would you get some more ice from the fridge for me?'

I'll do my good deed, Laura thought as she padded round the perimeter of the room, avoiding the swaying bodies massed in the centre, and then I'll go.

The kitchen was tiny, and the refrigerator was sited in the passage leading to it. Laura retrieved the ice tray and carried it over to the sink, taking a bowl down from the shelf above for the cubes.

But it seemed that instead of merely freezing, the ice had been glued into its containers, and Laura tried the hot tap, the handle of a knife and finally the back of a tablespoon, before, as luck would have it, all the cubes gave up the struggle together, crashing into the sink in a slithery mass, while one escapee made it to the floor and shot across the room.

Where it would melt, Laura thought crossly, and gave vent to a pungent expletive.

From behind her, a man's voice said amusedly, 'I knew you couldn't be nearly as refined as you look.'

She jumped. 'I didn't hear you,' she said, feeling foolish.

'I doubt if you'd hear the start of World War Three above that racket.' He came to stand beside her. 'Let me.' He scooped up the cubes in the sink and deposited them in the waiting bowl, in one deft movement.

Laura felt more ham-fisted then ever. 'Thank you,' she said rather stiffly. 'Perhaps you could take them in for me.'

'Gladly.' He picked up the bowl, but when she turned back to the sink with the recalcitrant cube melting in her hand, he was still there.

He said, 'You can't be Julie,' and she felt herself flush at the incredulous note in his voice. It was obvious what he was thinking—Edward liked sparkle and flash in his women, not pale, thin nonentities with straight tawny hair.

'No,' Laura said shortly. 'Julie is very dark, and very pretty, just as you'd expect.'

'Fantastic,' he said lightly. 'Perhaps you'll introduce me. I've been away for a few weeks, and I have some catching up to do.'

'Actually, I was just about to leave.' Laura dried her hands on a towel.

'Yes, I thought you were running away, when you left the room just now,' he remarked. 'You had the air of a fugitive. Although it wasn't a total surprise to find you in here, surrounded by ice.'

She felt the swift burn of irritation at the mockery in his voice, but she didn't let it show. Years of Celia had taught her not to rise too often to the bait.

All the same, she found herself wondering about him. He was a friend of Edward, obviously, but rather older than the usual run of them—thirty or more, she would have hazarded a guess, wearing the ubiquitous denim jeans as if they were a second skin, with the crisp white shirt accentuating the darkness of his skin.

She said levelly, 'Just doing my hostess a little favour. But I have to work in the morning, so late night parties are out.'

'Something tells me they were never in.' The corner of his mouth twisted slightly. He moved aside, waving her past with an oddly courtly gesture. 'You'd better make your escape while you can.'

Laura thought so too. This brief confrontation had thoroughly un-nerved her. She found herself thinking about it all the way back to her small bed-sitter, remembering with sudden warmth, the way the grey eyes had watched her.

He'd followed her, she realised with a certain bewilderment, and he'd made her feel—what? Special?

It was a prosaic way of describing the myriad emotions which had assailed her during those few moments.

She gave herself a mental shake. She was being ridiculous, reading too much into the situation. It was probably his party piece—seeking out the obvious wallflowers, and exerting a fraction of his charm on them. It was nothing to get excited about.

But there was no way she could rationalise the great leap of her heart the following day when she emerged from the elegant Georgian front door behind which the Farr Cordon Bleu school hid its endeavours, and found him waiting there.

Of course, she told herself, as he began to walk towards her, that did not mean he was waiting for her. It could all be an amazing coincidence.

She heard herself say inanely, 'What are you doing here?'

'I've come to see if last night's ice has melted.' He took her arm as if they'd known each other for years, she thought dazedly. 'It's too late for lunch, and too early for dinner, so may I offer you some afternoon tea?'

'I bet you never touch it.' She felt as if she was in a dream.

'Then you'd be wrong.' He was urging her along quite briskly in the chill autumn air, making her match her steps to his long stride. 'There's a hotel just round the corner where they make quite amazing sandwiches.'

They made cakes too, Laura discovered, and provided a big log fire in their lounge to eat them by. She thought, 'In a moment, I'll wake up. But not yet—please not yet.'

As she poured the tea, she said weakly, 'This is ridiculous. We don't even know each other's names.'

He said, 'You're Laura Caswell. Didn't Julie tell you that I was asking about you?'

She shook her head. 'Julie has no classes today. I—I haven't seen her.'

The grey eyes met hers enigmatically. 'That's probably just as well. She might have tried to warn you off.'

'Is there any reason why she should?' She noted with relief that her hand wasn't shaking as she passed him the cup.

'None that I can think of.' He lifted one shoulder in a shrug. 'But she tried to warn me.'

'About me?' Laura felt warmth in her cheeks. 'But there's nothing—I mean what could she say . . .'

He gave her a dry look. 'That you're not an easy lay.' He watched sardonically as the colour in Laura's face deepened hectically. 'I managed to assure her that my intentions are honourable.'

She moistened her lips with the tip of her tongue. 'I—I don't understand.'

'It's quite simple,' he said, 'I'm a painter. I'd like to paint you. That's all.'

She put her cup down on the table. 'I see—it's all a joke.'

'It's perfectly serious.' He frowned at her. 'Why should I be joking?'

'Because I'm not beautiful,' Laura said, looking him straight in the eye. 'I'm not even pretty. I'm the last person any artist would choose as a model.'

'You make it sound very decadent.' He sounded amused. 'But it isn't. I don't want to paint you in the nude, if that's what's worrying you.'

She bit her lip. 'It isn't.'

'Well then?'

'I told you. You didn't answer me.'

'You mean that little diatribe about your lack of physical charm?' He gave her an exasperated look. 'I want to paint you, Miss Caswell—not enter you in Miss World. You have a quality I've been looking for. And

I'm not asking for favours. I'll pay you the going professional rate.'

'But you don't know whether I'd be any good as a model,' she protested.

'You don't wriggle or twitch,' he said, 'You've been perfectly tranquil until a few minutes ago. You can be still, and I can teach you to give me what else I want.'

She looked down at her hands. 'And what's that?'

'Something I spotted as soon as I saw you at the party,' he said. 'You were on your own, but you didn't mind. You'd discovered how to be solitary, and it's that quality of loneness that I want in this painting.' He paused. 'Satisfied?'

She said slowly, 'You make it sound like a compliment, but I don't think it is.'

'Wait until you see the painting,' he said. 'And then judge.' He picked up one of the plates and handed it to her. 'Smoked salmon?'

She wasn't hungry, but she took one. 'I still don't know your name.'

He paused. 'It's Jason Wingard.' She thought there was something almost challenging about the way he looked at her.

She said penitently. 'Should I have heard of you? I'm afraid I don't know very much about painting . . .'

He grinned suddenly, showing white teeth. 'Very few people do. And I'm not a name to be reckoned with yet, although I do have some paintings in an exhibition— the Vallora Gallery.' He gave her a questioning look. 'Does that make me slightly more respectable?'

'It sounds quite impressive.' Laura drank some of her cooling tea. 'What would you want me to wear for this picture?'

'Anything you like,' he said. 'The things you wore to the party for preference.' He helped himself to the sandwiches. 'Do I take it that you agree? That you will pose for me?'

She said, 'If that's what you want, then—yes.'

'Good,' he said laconically. 'I'll be in touch.' He leaned back in his chair, stretching his long legs in front of him. He sent her a mocking glance. 'Don't look so shattered. It won't be the ordeal you imagine. Now, eat something before you collapse. Models need stamina.'

'So do cooks.' Laura helped herself to a piece of rich dark fruit cake.

'You're not a very good advertisement for your craft,' he said lazily. 'You're much too thin.'

She shrugged. 'It's all too easy to put on a lot of weight, if you're not careful.'

'So—you're always careful.' The grey eyes studied her. 'Aren't you ever tempted to break out and do something utterly reckless?'

She began to laugh suddenly. 'I think I've just done exactly that.'

He said softly, 'You can always change your mind.'

But Laura knew with utter certainty that she would not do anything of the kind.

There was a throb of excitement deep inside her which could not even be dispelled by a warning from Julie, who tackled her the following day.

'Of all the men at the party,' she mourned, 'you have to get involved with him.'

'Don't you like him?' Laura was surprised. 'I thought he was a friend of Edward's.'

Julie moved her shoulders dismissively. 'They're acquainted, but I wouldn't rate it any higher than that,' she said flatly. 'No-one, but no-one gets to know Jason Wingard well. He's always been a mystery man—talks about his work, but never about himself or his family, if he has one. In fact, he never mentions anyone belonging to him—as if he exists in a vacuum or something. He just arrived on the scene a couple of years ago, and that's as much as anyone knows.'

'Is he married?' Laura tried to keep her voice casual.

'He doesn't give that impression but who knows?' Julie shook her head. 'But that doesn't mean there aren't women,' she added, rather grimly. 'Because there are. But even they only get to share his bed, certainly not his life, and some of them have ended up really hurt. Oh, Laura, are you sure you know what you're doing?'

'He wants to paint me, not carve another notch on the bedpost,' Laura reassured her.

'I suppose he told you so himself.' Julie cast her dark eyes up to heaven. 'Laurie, you're so naïve about these things. So innocent. I suppose that's what he finds attractive. It's a rare quality these days.'

By the time she presented herself at the studio Jason rented in a converted warehouse by the river, all Laura's original qualms about the situation had intensified quite alarmingly, but the studio itself was something of a reassurance.

There were windows on two sides and an additional large skylight in the sloping roof, so that light poured in at all angles. There were the pervading odours of oil paint, linseed and turpentine in the air, yet the place wasn't nearly as cluttered as Laura had expected. It was clean and neat and apparently well organised, the canvases stacked in racks against the walls.

Jason greeted her impatiently. 'You're late.'

Almost before she finished unfastening her coat, he had taken it from her shoulders, his glance scanning the flare of her dark brown wool skirt, and its matching highnecked sweater. 'Is that what you're going to wear?'

'If you like,' she said nervously. 'Although I brought the other things.' She indicated the small case waiting by the door.

'Then change,' he ordered. He walked away from her to the small dais, and began altering the angle of the high-backed Victorian armchair which occupied it in front of a long burgundy velvet curtain. 'And hurry up,' he threw over his shoulder. 'Neither of us has all day. There's a changing area in the corner.'

The changing area was basic—a chair and a long mirror behind a screen. Laura put on the full-sleeved black blouse, and taffeta patchwork skirt she'd worn at the party, and ran a tentative comb through her hair. She felt as shy emerging from the sheltering screen as if she had been in the nude, she reflected wryly.

On the dais, Jason was businesslike as he instructed her in the pose he wanted. She was to sit on the floor, her legs tucked under her, leaning back against the broad seat of the chair, and resting one arm on it. It was a comfortable position to hold on the face of it, but Laura suspected she would soon get tired and cramped. She found it distinctly un-nerving to have Jason touch her, altering the position of her head, the turn of her body by what seemed infinitesimal degrees, but he was as impersonal as if he'd been re-arranging an ornament on a shelf.

He said once abruptly, 'This taffeta drapes well,' but apart from that there was silence between them.

At last he perched on a stool, holding a drawing board, his face intent as he began a series of sketches, changing his position constantly round the dais so that he could draw every angle of her.

At last he said, 'Okay, you can rest now. We'll have some coffee.' He nodded towards a sidetable where a kettle and the other necessary paraphernalia reposed. 'The stuff's over there.'

Laura got stiffly to her feet, shaking the creases out of her skirt. 'Do I make it?'

He shrugged, 'You're the cook.'

She said lightly, 'You don't need a diploma to unite some instant coffee with boiling water and powdered milk.'

As she spooned granules into the waiting beakers, she was aware of Jason prowling restlessly around, picking up his sketch pad and staring frowningly at the results.

She said, 'How's it going?'

'Not well,' he said shortly. 'You need to relax more. You're sitting there as if you've been carved out of wood.'

Laura bit her lip. 'I'm sorry. I told you it would probably be no good.'

'Yes, you told me.' He took the beaker she proffered. The grey eyes studied her levelly. 'So—what is it, Laura Caswell? Why are you so uptight?'

'I'm not,' she denied instantly. 'Although this is—a new situation for me.'

'What is? Posing—or simply being alone with a man?'

A dull flush rose in her face. 'That's not fair.'

'Very little is,' he said. He went on watching her speculatively. 'I suspect I have Julie to thank for this sudden rigidity.'

Laura jumped, nearly spilling her coffee. 'I don't know what you mean.'

'Of course you do.' He reached forward and took the beaker from her, setting it carefully aside. He was smiling faintly as he pulled her into his arms. His dark face seemed to swim before her eyes, and she closed them quickly, her heart thudding painfully under the silky shirt.

The kiss was brief, his mouth warm and terrifyingly sensuous. She was trembling, melting against him as he lifted his head.

He said laconically, 'Now that I've made the token pass, perhaps we can get on with some serious work.'

She gave him a dazed look, 'I don't understand . . .'

He smiled derisively. 'Isn't that what you've been afraid of ever since you arrived? Isn't that why you've stiffened into stone every time I've come near you?'

She swallowed, unable to think of a single thing to

say that wouldn't make her sound more foolish than she already felt.

He said, 'I intend to paint you, Miss Caswell, not seduce you, whatever impression Julie may have given. Now, if you'll drink your coffee, we'll start again.'

All she had to do was leave. Walk past him to the door and be gone. Yet she did not do so. She found herself picking up the beaker, sipping the coffee, clutching at normality again, trying to forget the devastating effect of his kiss.

There was a charged silence between them which she felt impelled, at last, to break. She said, 'I went to the gallery to see your pictures.'

He gave her a sardonic look. 'Did you now? So— what did you think of them?'

She hesitated. 'I think they frightened me a little. They seemed harsh—savage even. I didn't really understand them.'

'You seem to have understood enough,' he said with a faint shrug. 'Are you afraid I'm going to paint you in that way?'

'Perhaps.' She stared down at her coffee. 'Most of them have been sold. You must be pleased.'

'Not particularly. Pleased to be rid of them, maybe. They belong to a bad time in my life.' He moved restlessly. 'Shall we get started?' He saw the lingering uncertainty in her face, and said more gently, 'The bad time's over. I'm out of that particular tunnel—for good. Now, will you come back and take up the pose?'

It was easier this time. She sank down into it, leaning back against the chair, composing herself, watching him set up the prepared canvas, and begin to work, wondering about this man, and the bad time in his life which had produced those raw explosions of colour which she had seen at the Vallora Gallery. And discovering, with a kind of shock, just how much she wanted to know all these things about him.

At last he said, 'We'll leave it for today. Can you come back tomorrow?'

'Yes.' She stretched aching muscles. 'Can I look?'

'Not yet—there's nothing to see.' A quick smile took any sense of rebuff from the words. 'But it's there, Laura Caswell. It's coming.'

She went the next day, and the day after that, until the studio became as familiar to her as the gleaming kitchens she worked in, or her own tiny flat. Julie was still issuing dire mutterings, but Laura ignored them.

Looking back with hindsight she could see that she was already caught, for better or worse. That if there had been no portrait, no excuse for her presence, she would still have been there somehow, because she had begun to need to be with him.

The strain of posing, the aches, the pins and needles were all worth it for the moments when they relaxed over a cup of coffee, and he talked to her. Not about himself, Julie had been right about that at least. But then Laura had never been used to talk about herself either, yet now under the pressure of his almost casual questioning, she found she was revealing more and more about her childhood, the death of her parents, her life under her uncle's care. Found she was formulating viewpoints, and discovering things about herself that she had hardly been aware existed.

Layers of reserve were being peeled away, she realised with a little shiver when she was alone again, lying sleepless in her flat, staring at the ceiling. And what he discovered under those layers was presumably going into the portrait he still would not let her see.

It troubled her to realise too how completely Jason seemed to have taken possession of her consciousness. She thought about him all the time, remembering every word, every glance. Remembering with terrifying emphasis that brief, searing kiss.

It had never been repeated. There was nothing in his

manner to suggest she was any more to him than the subject he had chosen to paint, a collection of light and shade to be reproduced on canvas. Any interest he displayed was professional, not personal.

Occasionally, while she'd been at the studio, there had been telephone calls, and she knew by the intimate lowering of his voice that they were from women—or perhaps one woman. She tried not to listen, not to speculate, telling herself it was none of her business, trying to ignore the gnawings of a jealousy she had no right to feel. He had his life. She had hers. When the portrait was finished it was doubtful whether their paths would ever cross again, and it was stupid to feel so desolate at the prospect. After all, he was still a comparative stranger.

Reasoning with herself was simple. Acting reasonably, calling her emotions to order was less so.

And when in the middle of the second week he told her abruptly that the picture was almost finished and he wouldn't need her any more, she almost blanked out with shock. It was like having a lifeline severed, and she hadn't realised it would be so soon—so soon . . .

She came to stand beside him at the easel and looked at the portrait. She stood for a long time in silence, looking at herself, seeing what he had seen perhaps only for a moment across the crowded room at the party— her stillness, her sense of total isolation. In its way, it was more disturbing that the pictures she'd flinched from in the gallery. She felt defenceless, utterly vulnerable.

'Nothing to say?' His grey eyes pierced her. She tried to smile.

'What are you going to call it? "Portrait of an Unknown Girl"?'

'No,' he said ' "Laura alone".'

He took her by the shoulders, drawing her towards

him, and she went unresistingly, lifting her face blindly
for his kiss. Her hands clung to his shoulders, her
mouth parting under the dizzying pressure of his, and
her body swayed pliantly against him.

His kiss deepened hungrily, making demands she had
never realised existed. Nothing had prepared her for the
shivering rush of need it evoked. She could not think
any more, only feel, her senses exulting as his long
fingers caressed the slender column of her spine.

The world was melting and she was dissolving in its
sweetness, his lean, hard body against hers the only
certainty.

He lifted her into his arms and carried her to the big
chair on the dais. She lay across him, her hands
feverishly touching his hair, stroking his face as he
kissed her again and again. When his fingers released
the buttons on her shirt, one by one, she had no
thought of any kind of protest. His touch on her skin
was a miracle. Until that moment, she thought, she had
never known what it was to be alive. The cool, guarded
girl of the portrait had never existed.

She gasped as his restless hands uncovered her small
high breasts, caressing the rosy peaks into a torment of
desire.

She heard a voice she hardly recognised as her own
sobbing, 'Please—oh, please . . .' and in that moment
felt him draw back, as if her words had broken some
kind of spell.

Her lashes flew open. She stared up at him. There
was a faint flush along the high cheekbones, his mouth
was compressed almost grimly, and his eyes were as
dark as night as he looked back at her.

He said quietly, 'Am I the first?'

She whispered, 'Yes' and realised with a kind of
dread, that he was letting her go, putting her away from
him. She reared up, winding her arms round his neck,
pulling him down to her again, her lips seeking his in

innocent abandon, trying to overcome the hesitation
she sensed in him.

For a moment, he held back, then with a smothered
groan, he capitulated, crushing her against him with a
new fierce demand, possessing the softness of her
mouth with a kind of controlled savagery.

When she could speak, she murmured, 'Don't send
me away, Jason. Promise me that you won't.'

He said hoarsely, 'God knows I should—but I don't
think I can.' His arms tightened, lifting her, setting her
on her feet, as he rose lithely to stand beside her. She
looked up at him, her eyes widening in bewilderment,
and his face softened. He lifted a hand and caressed the
curve of her chin.

'Not here,' he told her softly. 'Not like this—for your
first time with a man. Trust me, Laura.'

'Yes.' She felt no sense of shame at her total
commitment. She loved him. She wanted to belong to
him. It was as simple as that. She'd heard that was how
it happened sometimes, but she'd never thought it
would ever apply to herself.

There was no past. There would probably be no
future. There was only the present, and when he took
her hand, she went with him.

She'd hardly been aware of her surroundings. There
had been wine, she remembered, and the coolness of
clean sheets making her shiver slightly as she lay and
watched him draw the curtains, closing out the daylight
and the world. He undressed without haste. Everything
he did was unhurried, she discovered, as he took her
with him on that slow endless journey into pleasure,
controlling the power of his body to bring her to total
acceptance, total passionate surrender.

Afterwards, she supposed she must have slept.
When she opened her eyes, he was lying beside her
propped on one elbow, watching her. He smiled at
her, sliding a hand down her body, reminding her of

that final, incredible urgency which had possessed them both.

He said, 'I'm going to paint you again.' His lips brushed the beginnings of her own smile. ' "Laura fulfilled".'

In the darkness, Laura lay alone, torturing herself with memories. It was madness to think of these things, to let herself remember how it had been with them, the wild sensual magic his hands and mouth had always engendered for her.

And it was shaming to realise that he had lost none of his power over her, even though she knew what he was, even though the bitter truths of their relationship had been brought home to her a long time ago.

Especially when, now, he was with Celia.

The storm was passing. Above the muted rumble of the thunder, she heard the sound of the car engine starting up, saw the glare of headlights sweep her window.

She thought, 'He's gone' and tried with a kind of desperation to be glad.

CHAPTER SIX

As she walked down Burngate the following morning, it seemed to Laura as if the previous night's storm had been a figment of her imagination. The day was cloudless and sunny, and even in town the air seemed to sparkle.

Just beyond the restaurant, she could see Alan's car still forlornly waiting, a parking ticket tucked vindictively under one of the windscreen wipers.

Something to add to the hangover he was undoubtedly suffering, Laura thought wryly.

On the pretext of shopping, she'd managed to escape from the house before Celia came downstairs. She would have to face her sometime, and the barbed remarks and inferences which would be coming her way, but not yet. Not until she was fully back in charge of her emotions.

She rang the bell at the restaurant's side door, and before the sound had died away, the door had opened, and Bethany's smiling face appeared.

'Come in.' She tugged Laura over the step. 'What a morning we're having. 'The 'phone has hardly stopped ringing. We have bookings until the end of next week. It's fantastic.'

'Oh, Beth, I'm delighted for you.' Laura hugged her. 'But you thoroughly deserve it. Your husband is an inspired cook.'

'He's an inspired everything,' Bethany said demurely.

Superman, who was waiting in the flat upstairs, turned out to be medium height with brown hair, and smiling eyes, and Laura liked him at once.

They sat at the oval table in the window overlooking

the street, drinking coffee and nibbling at homemade shortbread while they caught up on the news of mutual acquaintances. After a while, Mike excused himself and vanished down to the kitchen to start work on some soup.

'He's so happy,' Bethany said fondly. 'This was quite a gamble for us in a number of ways, but one of his aunts bought us some premium bonds as a wedding present, and we actually won. Oh, not the big prize, or anything like it,' she added hastily. 'But enough to make us feel that if we ever were going to work for ourselves it had to be now or never. But what about you, Laura? Did you ever make use of your diploma?'

Laura hesitated. 'To a certain extent. I help out at Caswells when anything special is required in the way of food, but that's all.'

Bethany was silent for a moment, her frank blue eyes studying her friend. She said, 'It's probably none of my business, but rumour had it that you'd got married.'

Laura bit her lip. 'I did.' She forced a smile. 'It—it didn't work out, and we're now divorced.'

'Oh,' Bethany said helplessly. 'Laura, I'm really sorry. I don't know what to say.'

Laura shrugged slightly. 'That's all right. I'm over it now.'

Am I? Oh God, am I?

'Did I ever meet him?' Bethany persisted, and Laura shook her head.

'He was an artist, then. His name's Jason Wingard,' she added flatly.

'Wingard?' Bethany frowned. 'Odd—that name rings a bell.'

'I expect it does,' Laura said drily. 'Look at last night's cheques, and you'll find it among them.'

'He was in here last night?' Bethany's brows vanished almost into her hair.

Laura nodded. 'It was quite a family party.'

'Then it was one of those civilised divorces?'

Laura wanted to scream, 'No—it tore me to pieces, and still does,' but instead she said lightly, 'I suppose you could say that.' She changed the subject abruptly. 'What happened to Julie? Do you ever see her these days?'

'The last I heard of her, she'd gone abroad.' Bethany reached for the coffee pot, and refilled the cups. While she was adding cream. Laura looked idly down into the street.

Alan still hadn't moved his car, she noticed, and there was no sign of him anywhere. If he wasn't careful, it might be towed away.

Burngate itself was relatively quiet for the time of day, with little traffic and few pedestrians. A boy, his hair dyed like a cockatoo's and aggressively lacquered, strode along the pavement, attracting scandalised looks from more conventional shoppers, and Laura smiled to herself as he sidestepped to let a girl with a pushchair walk past him to the window of the estate agent's opposite.

Suddenly she could feel the blood drumming in her head and felt her chest tightening almost unbearably.

'Laura.' Bethany jumped up. 'My God, love, what is it? You're ill. Put your head down—that's it. Now, try and breathe deeply, but don't force it.'

Laura obeyed, aware that the room was swimming nauseatingly round her. Within seconds Mike had appeared with a glass of water, summoned by Bethany's urgent call. Between them, they got Laura to lie down on the sofa. She drank some of the water, and gradually the room stopped revolving.

She said at last, 'I'm sorry. I feel a complete fool. It must be lack of sleep. The storm kept me awake last night and . . .'

Mike had discreetly vanished again. Bethany took her hand gently. 'You're not a fool, love, and neither am I. You looked as if you'd seen a ghost just then. What is it?'

Laura gave her a wan smile. 'No ghost—very much flesh and blood. At least, I think so. I could have made a mistake.'

'Then who is it, for heaven's sake?' Bethany dragged forward a chair and sat down.

Laura was silent for a long moment. She said, 'I suppose the simplest way to say it is—my husband's mistress and one of his children.'

There was a charged silence, then Bethany said, 'You're joking—surely——' then caught herself quickly, 'No, it isn't a joke. You don't make jokes about things like that. But Laura, my God, you said—one of his children. You mean he has more than one?'

'One more that I know about,' Laura said wearily. 'An older boy. I suppose he'll be at school now.'

There was another long pause, then Bethany said gently, 'You don't have to say any more if you don't want to, but if it would help to talk about it, then I'm more than ready to listen.'

'It might help at that.' Laura spoke half to herself. 'I've managed to keep it all locked away all this time, because I really thought I'd never have to see him again. But now, he's back, and obviously she's still with him.' She gave a little choked laugh. 'Although God knows why. He certainly never treated her very well. He turned his back on her to marry me, even if that was only a temporary aberration, and now he's started an affair with my cousin Celia.'

Bethany whistled soundlessly. She said caustically, 'The gentleman gets around. Why the hell did you marry him?'

'Because I fell in love.' Laura looked down at her hands, clenched together in her lap. 'Head over heels, helplessly, deliriously in love—the kind they write poetry about.'

Only in our case, she thought, all the rhymes were wrong.

She began to tell Bethany about it, going back to the beginning to the time when she and Jason had become lovers, and the endless painful three weeks which had followed when she neither saw him nor heard from him.

All she could tell herself, all she could believe was that Julie had been right after all about him. That maybe his insistence on painting her had been nothing but an elaborate ploy to get her into bed, and that, having succeeded, he wanted nothing more from her.

She reminded herself over and over again that she wasn't the first it had happened to, and she certainly wouldn't be the last, but it did nothing to dispel the hurt lying like a stone inside her.

And then one day, he was waiting for her outside the school, just like it had been that first time. There was something watchful in the way he looked at her, something contained, as if he wasn't altogether sure of his welcome, but she was holding back too, because her first impulse had been to run to him, and fling herself into his arms.

He made no attempt to touch her or kiss her. He said abruptly, 'Have you finished for the day? We need to talk.'

'If you're worried,' she said, colour rising in her face, 'about what happened between us, then there's no need. It's—all right.'

For a moment he stared at her as if he didn't know what she was talking about, then he gave a short laugh. 'Do you know, I never gave it a thought. But it would have made absolutely no difference.' He took her hand and they began to walk slowly along the street together. He said, 'I want you to marry me, Laura.'

'Marry?' The breath seemed to stop in her throat. 'But—why?'

He shrugged slightly. 'For the usual reasons, I

suppose—and more.' His fingers tightened round hers. 'When I recognised that solitary quality in you, it was because I possess it myself. It isn't a good way for the human animal to be. We need mutual support, warmth, comfort.'

'And love?' she said.

He said drily, 'I thought that was what I was talking about. If you mean physical compatibility, then we seem to have that too. Isn't that enough? Needs in both of us that the other can satisfy?'

There was a silence, then she said helplessly, 'I can't believe that you're serious.'

'How can I convince you?' The grey eyes were full of laughter suddenly. 'Do you want me to go down on one knee in the street?' He sank gracefully down in front of her, holding her hand ageinst his heart. It's beat sounded strong and unflurried, but her own pulses were going off like rockets. He said, 'Darling Laura—be mine.'

'Oh, get up.' She tugged at his shoulder. 'People are looking at us.'

'Why not? We're a handsome couple. And I'm not moving from this spot until I get an answer to my honourable proposal. Don't be alone any more, Laura. Come and live with me instead.'

It was madness, and she knew it, but it was also what she wanted more than life itself.

She said on a note of laughter, 'Yes—oh, yes.'

She was amazed at the speed with which it was accomplished. Her course had only another couple of weeks to run, and then they would be married.

She said doubtfully, 'So soon?'

'There's nothing to wait for. We need a licence and two witnesses, that's all.'

'But isn't there anyone you'd like to be there?'

'No.' The reply was clipped and definite. 'And you?'

She was hesitant. 'I should tell Uncle Martin. He's

been my guardian ever since my parents died.'

'Tell him then.' His eyes challenged her. 'Or are you afraid that he'll forbid the banns?'

'No.' She shook her head, although she didn't really know what Uncle Martin's reaction would be. He'd told her since childhood that she would always have a home with him, almost as if he expected her to be doomed to everlasting spinsterhood. And perhaps he did at that, because she was certainly no match for Celia in looks.

But the situation was out of her hands, because when she telephoned the house, Mrs Fraser told her that Mr Caswell was abroad on a marketing trip, and unlikely to be back before the end of the month. The usual faint curtness in her tone did not encourage Laura to confide in her.

So by the time her uncle returned, the marriage was a *fait accompli*, and her wedding ring no longer felt alien on her hand.

She rang him at the works to tell him the news, and ask if she could bring Jason down for the weekend to meet him. Her words were greeted initially by a stunned silence, and then with an explosion of rage.

'Married?' His voice stormed at her. 'Married? You must be out of your mind. Who is this fellow?'

She said quietly, 'The man I love. Uncle Martin— please be happy for me.'

There had been another long silence, then he'd muttered an ungracious assent to their visit and rung off, leaving Laura mystified, and more than a little troubled. She tried to comfort herself that the sight of her obvious happiness would mollify him.

But it hadn't turned out like that at all. In fact the visit had been pretty much of a disaster from start to finish. Jason and her uncle had descended from cool civility to a wary antagonism, until Laura felt like the buffer state between two nations preparing to declare war.

She was bewildered by their reaction to each other. Alone with Jason in their room, she tried tentatively to justify her uncle's reactions.

'He's always been so good to me, so generous,' she told him unhappily. 'Getting married like this—he must feel as if I've slapped him in the face.'

Jason was sitting on the edge of the bed, unbuttoning his shirt. He gave her a wry look. 'So—you think if we'd waited, asked his permission, had the ceremony in the local church with him to give you away—that would have made all the difference?'

'It might,' she said.

He shook his head, shrugging off his shirt. As always, the sight of his lean body turned her mouth dry with excitement. 'You're fooling yourself, my darling. There's no way I could ever be an acceptable husband in your uncle's eyes, for all kinds of reasons.'

After lunch on Sunday when Jason had gone for a walk, she found out what some of those reasons were.

'He's no good,' her uncle had said brutally as they faced each other.' He's a down-at-heel artist with an eye to the main chance, and in you he's got a meal ticket for life. That's all you'll ever be to him, Laura. I'm surprised your own commonsense didn't tell you that.'

She said fiercely, 'It's not true. You have no right to say that.'

'I have every right, my dear.' He looked older suddenly. 'I'm very fond of you, Laura. I've always tried to do my best for you. Your marriage has been a shock—a blow and I won't deny it. Why you've admitted yourself that you know nothing about him— his family, his background, and these things matter, although you may not think so.' He paused. 'Naturally, he's aware that you receive an income from the company under your father's will.'

'I told him, yes, but it isn't really important. Jason is going to be a success in his own right. His paintings sell.' She tried to smile. 'You make him sound like a fortune hunter, and me like some nineteenth-century heiress.'

'Joke about it as much as you want.' He stared at her, his chin jutting angrily. 'But I tell you it's the Caswell name that attracted him to you, whatever romantic dreams you may be harbouring. He probably thought you were Celia,' he added sharply, and she flinched.

'That's an awful thing to say.'

'I'm trying to be realistic—something that's apparently beyond you. But I'm warning you, Laura, honeymoons don't last for ever.'

And hers, she thought, was over almost before it had begun. She tried to dismiss everything that Uncle Martin had said from her mind, but it wasn't that easy, she discovered. Some of it lingered in unexpected corners, festering there, making her wonder—doubt even.

She and Jason had a joint savings account. They were living at his small flat, making do, planning for a bigger place or even a small house, so there was no reason in the world for her to have snapped at him when he asked her casually once if there'd been any provision for an increase in her income on her marriage.

'Of course not.' There were two spots of colour on her cheekbones. 'My father was only the junior partner in the company. My cousin's the wealthy heiress, not me.'

Even in her own ears the words sounded barbed and accusing. Jason had stared at her for a long moment, his eyes narrowing, then without another word he'd got up and gone out.

He'd come back very late, sliding into bed beside her where she lay, pretending to be asleep. But he hadn't been deceived for an instant. He'd pulled her into his arms with a force that brooked no denial, and made slow, fierce, calculating love to her until she was pliant, mindless with the promise and torment of ecstasy ruthlessly withheld.

'Ask me,' he'd said savagely against her lips, his hands grazing her with delicious cruelty. 'Beg me, you little bitch.'

She had no pride, no will to resist. Her plea was whispered thickly from her throat, and his response was almost a snarl as he drove them both over the edge of passion to a culmination of shattering pleasure.

A long time afterwards, lying with her head pillowed on his shoulder, she told him shyly how wonderful it had been.

His voice was almost laconic. 'As your paid stud, I try to give satisfaction.'

'Jason,' she protested, moving sharply, lifting herself on one elbow to look down at him. 'I didn't mean that. I didn't mean anything . . .'

'No?' The dark face was enigmatic. 'Then that's all right.'

But it wasn't, as she realised afterwards. It was the first crack in the fragile shell of her security.

Not long after that she had discovered she was going to have a baby. She'd expected Jason to be as thrilled as she was, yet his reaction had been muted, almost negative.

Needing reassurance, she'd asked, 'Jason—you're not sorry.'

He took her in his arms, his face frankly rueful. 'No—but I hadn't intended it to happen so soon, and now may not be the best time,' he'd added, half to himself.

'Why?' She was instantly concerned, knowing that another exhibition was being planned.

He kissed her lightly, 'Nothing that need concern you. You concentrate on looking after yourself, and our baby.'

As her body adapted itself for the coming child, Laura found her personality had changed too, and not for the better either. In those first months along with morning sickness, she found herself increasingly weepy and aggressive.

And the fact that Jason was working so hard in the studio didn't help. He'd had his portrait of her framed, and she thought 'Laura alone' as she stared at it, tears dripping from the end of her nose.

A couple of times she'd telephoned him at the studio and there'd been no reply, and this had puzzled her. When he returned in the evening, she'd probed gently asking how his work had gone, only to be told brusquely, 'Fine' in a way which discouraged further enquiries.

But it was when he began disappearing for longer and longer periods during the evenings that she began to get seriously disturbed over the situation.

On the doctor's advice, they had ceased to make love until Laura's pregnancy was firmly established, but that didn't mean she'd stopped needing comfort and affection, all the things he'd talked about when he married her, and as the days passed, her feelings sharpened into grievance. She tried to find out where he was going, but it was like running headlong into a brick wall. Her questions were neatly turned aside, and she was left none the wiser.

At last, her sense of grievance spilled over into a row. She'd been feeling slightly off colour all day, and when after their meal, Jason stood up reaching for his coat, she'd said sharply, 'Where are you going?'

'I have to go out.'

'So I've noticed. You're making quite a habit of it.' Her voice was bitter.

He gave her a long, considering look. 'Being married doesn't mean spending every minute of every day together,' he told her evenly.

'And it doesn't mean I want to be left on my own night after night either,' she said angrily. 'I'm having your baby in case you've forgotten.'

'I'm hardly likely to do that.' His own voice was acid. 'Not only am I not allowed to touch you, but I get vivid descriptions of all the sufferings you're being subjected to.'

She'd just been going to tell him she wasn't feeling well, and ask him not to leave her, but at that she stiffened. 'I'm sorry. I didn't realise I was being a bore.'

'You're not,' he said. 'Just a little self-obsessed, but I suppose it's natural.'

'You're damned right it is,' she said off the top of her voice. 'Particularly when I have a husband who does a vanishing trick nearly every evening. Why won't you tell me where you're going? Why does it have to be such a secret?'

His mouth was hard and set. 'Because I don't want you to be involved. Anyway, I haven't time to argue about that now. I have to go.'

'But I want to be involved.' She lifted her chin stubbornly. 'I'm your wife, Jason. I have a right to know about your life. You've got to tell me where you go.'

There was a long silence, then he sighed, lifting a shoulder in a brief defeated shrug. 'Very well, if you feel you have to know. I go to visit my father who is ill.'

She was stunned. Whatever she'd been expecting, it wasn't that.

She said weakly. 'Your father? But I thought you had no family . . . You've never mentioned . . .' She paused helplessly. 'And now you say you have a father living. Why didn't you tell me?'

He said curtly, 'Because I'd cut myself off from them, for reasons I'm not prepared to discuss with you. I never intended to have any contact with them again, so if you're cherishing ideas of a cosy circle waiting to welcome you into it, think again. It's not going to happen.'

'You haven't told them you're married?' She stared at him, and when he shook his head, she drew a quick furious breath. 'You're ashamed of me in some way.'

'You're talking like a fool,' he said coldly.

'I feel a fool.' Her hands clenched into fists. 'All this time, and no hint, no word. You said "them" so I take it you have a mother too.'

'Yes.' Just the quiet monosyllable, no attempt at explanation or elaboration.

'Brothers and sisters?'

'None—nor aunts, uncles or cousins. Are you satisfied now? Do you know enough?' Her voice had risen with her questions, and he was almost shouting in reply.

'Of course not. How could you have kept a thing like this from me?'

'Quite easily, under the circumstances.' His voice flattened. 'Understand this, Laura, the split with my parents is permanent, and the fact of our marriage makes not the slightest difference to that. If it were all to happen again, I would act in exactly the same way. And before you even ask—no, you may not come with me.' He shrugged into his coat. 'I'll be as quick as I can. You're looking tired. You'd better have an early night.'

She was left, staring at the closed door, unable to believe what had just passed between them. She couldn't even begin to guess at the nature of the rupture between them which had left Jason so bitter, but it frightened her just the same. She'd never dreamed how hard he could be, how unforgiving.

For a long time she sat, gazing into space, in front of the gently hissing gasfire, trying to come to terms with what had happened. She stirred at last, aware that she'd been sitting in an awkward position and her back was aching badly. She got up stiffly, preparing to clear the remains of their meal from the table, and a dull pain struck at her, making her clench her teeth. There was other discomfort too, and she knew with a sudden chill that she was bleeding.

She had to get help. Moving slowly and carefully, she made her way across the passage to the opposite flat. Lucinda, the West Indian girl who lived there with her husband answered the door, her smiling face sobering into concern as she looked at Laura.

'Hey, honey, this is no good.' Lucinda's arm went round her, supporting her. 'You come and lie down, while Henry 'phones for Dr Murdoch.'

Everything faded into a blue of pain and distress. She knew she was in an ambulance, became aware of flowered curtains and a high hard bed. Heard a girl's voice say, 'Just something to help you sleep, dear,' and felt the quick stab of an injection in her arm.

When she woke up Jason was there. His face was drawn and he needed a shave.

'How are you feeling?' His hand, warm and strong, covered hers. 'All right.' Her eyes searched his face. 'Jason—the baby?'

His silence gave her the answer she'd been expecting, and she sank back against the pillows, tears beginning to trickle down her face.

'He said, 'Laura, I've been talking to Dr Murdoch. He says when these things happen early like this, it can sometimes be for the best. He's been anxious about you from the beginning.' He lifted her hand to his lips. 'Don't cry, my darling ... Dr Murdoch says you're going to be fine, and there's little chance of anything like this happening again. We've just been unlucky this time.'

'Yes,' she said. She couldn't stop the tears, but inside she felt numb. The last twenty-four hours had been a nightmare, and it wasn't just the loss of the baby she had to adjust to.

She was allowed home the following day. Jason fetched her in a taxi and when they got to the house he carried her upstairs to their flat. There were flowers in a vase, and a home-baked sponge from Lucinda among the tea things on the neatly laid table, but thankfully nothing to remind her of her short-lived pregnancy. She hadn't begun to shop for the baby—almost as if she'd known, she thought wincing.

Jason made her lie on the sofa, and brought her tea. He said 'I phoned your uncle.'

'What did he say?'

'He was upset, naturally. He sent his love and asked if you wanted to go down and stay for a few days?'

'What did you tell him?'

'I said it was up to you.' He was silent for a moment. 'Perhaps a change of scene might do you good.'

'It would certainly stop me asking awkward questions,' she said coolly and deliberately.

'That too,' he agreed expressionlessly. They were antagonists again.

She looked down at her cup. 'Then perhaps it would be a good idea—for a few days.'

'I said you'd 'phone him later.'

'Yes.' They were talking like strangers, and there was nothing she could do to bridge the gulf, because he was a stranger. Anyone who could behave as if his parents had never existed had to be a stranger, not the man who'd taught her all the intimacies of passion. She felt a kind of desperation settling on her. She said 'I'll need some money.'

'Of course.' Another brief silence. 'I've had to draw on our account lately, quite heavily.'

She shrugged. 'It's our money.' She felt very tired. She put down her cup of cooling tea.

Martin Caswell sent a car to collect her and Jason

put her into it. His kiss was brief, but the look he gave her before he turned away was searching.

She sat staring out of the window, watching the suburbs fade with a guilty sense of relief. It was wrong to want to be going home like this, because her real home was with Jason, or should be, but she was thankful to be escaping even for a little while.

Her uncle's greeting was as warm as she could have wished. Her old room was waiting, as if she'd never been away, and even Mrs Fraser was almost cordial.

He even had his own doctor examine her, even though she protested that Dr Murdoch had given her a clean bill of health.

'You can't be too careful, my dear,' he brushed aside her objections. 'There might be some inherent weakness . . .'

But the new doctor was as optimistic as his colleague in London. He talked of 'bad luck' too, but assured Laura she was as strong as a horse. 'No reason why you shouldn't have half a dozen children, if you want,' he said. 'And don't leave it too long before you try again.'

We didn't try, Laura thought. The baby wasn't planned, or even particularly convenient. She wondered whether Jason would want to 'try again'. It didn't seem very likely.

She ate all the delicacies Mrs Fraser took the trouble to concoct and walked in the garden. She was afraid, she told herself. There was nothing the matter with her. She 'phoned Jason to tell him she wanted to come back, but there was no answer, neither from the flat nor the studio, even though she tried several times.

As soon as her uncle came home that evening, she knew there was something wrong. His greeting was subdued, his ruddy face unusually sombre. She supposed that something had happened at Caswells, and resolved to ask him about it over dinner, but the only reply she got was 'Not now, my dear, later.'

She made his coffee for him in the way that he liked it, and brought it to him with a brandy. He took them from her with a word of thanks, then said, 'Sit down, Laura, I have some things to say to you which I'm afraid are going to distress you.'

'About the company?'

He shook his head. 'About the man you married.' He paused, then said abruptly, 'I've been having some enquiries made about him, and I've learned something which will be a shock to you.'

Laura moistened her dry lips with the tip of her tongue. 'If it's the fact that his parents are alive . . .'

'It isn't.' He stared at her. 'I understood from you that he was an orphan, so it never occurred to me to have any checks made of that kind.'

She sat very still. 'What are these checks—these enquiries? Uncle Martin, you have no right. . . .'

'I have every right,' he said testily. 'You're my poor brother's child. Just because you've allowed yourself to be rushed into a disastrous marriage doesn't mean I have to wash my hands of you. You're a Caswell and your interests have to be protected.'

'By setting private detectives on to Jason.' A shiver of distaste went through her. 'I don't think I want to hear . . .'

'And I think you must.' His voice was inflexible. She had half-risen, and he gestered impatiently to her to sit down again. 'Believe me, child, I would never have done this if I hadn't believed it was essential. And even then, I might have held back if he hadn't started asking me for money.'

She was shaken to the core. 'Jason—asked you?'

He nodded. 'On more than one occasion. At first I complied for your sake, but his demands became excessive and arrogant, and that was when I decided to have him watched.'

She sat rigidly, watching him, unable to speak.

'I've received a number of reports from the agency I engaged to act for me, and my worst fears have been confirmed.' He shook his head heavily, 'Laura, your husband is supporting a mistress—a woman calling herself Clare Marshall. She has a child aged about three, and Jason Wingard's name appears on the birth certificate. She lives quite affluently, I understand, in a block of flats in Belgravia, and he has been visiting her regularly there since your marriage.'

Laura said, 'I—don't—believe it.'

'If you want proof, I can supply it.' The florid face was crumpled, pitying. 'There are the written reports—and photographs. On one occasion as he was leaving, the child called him "Daddy".' He paused. 'Apparently there is an unmistakable resemblance.'

He put the photographs into her hands and she looked at them. She wanted to say that photographs could be forged, but she couldn't find the words and anyway the pictures were obviously real.

The woman was dark, slim, attractive in her middle twenties. The child was Jason in miniature. In one photograph, Jason was carrying him in his arms towards a car—an Alfa Romeo, she noted in passing—and the likeness they shared made her heart turn over.

There was more damning evidence in the reports—'the subject' leaving their own tiny, unfashionable flat or his studio and being followed, dates, hours and destinations all meticulously listed. Among them, she saw brief visits to a West End clinic, usually measured in minutes, as if Jason had been establishing the alibi of the sick father to account for his actions.

She thought, 'I'm beginning to think like one of Uncle Martin's enquiry agents.'

Aloud, she said, 'This must have cost you a great deal of money.'

'The cost is immaterial,' he said. 'The essential thing was to show you the kind of man you had married. I imagine this woman has some money of her own. Your husband would hardly be able to support her in this kind of style merely on what he makes from the sale of his work, and whatever money he can scrounge from Caswells.'

'If this is his child, then he's morally and legally obliged to support him.' Laura hardly recognised her own voice. 'We can't blame him for that. And naturally, he'll want to see him sometimes. But why didn't he tell me there'd been this relationship?'

He said heavily, 'Because it's still going on, my dear. The latest reports state that the Marshall woman is pregnant—between four and five months, it's estimated.'

Laura said hoarsely, 'But that's not possible. It would mean . . .' She was unable to go on.

Martin Caswell nodded. 'It would mean the child had been conceived since Wingard's marriage to you.' There was a long pause. Then, 'Laura, my dear, I would have given a great deal to be able to keep this from you. But against the hurt you will inevitably suffer, I must balance the fact that you've been disgracefully insulted, and it cannot be allowed to continue. You do see that?'

She said, 'Yes.' But all she saw was images of Jason and this woman together, their bodies entwined. She made a little sound and pressed her hand against her mouth.

'Are you all right?' Martin Caswell got ponderously to his feet.

'I think I'd like to be alone for a while.' She rose. 'May I take these things to my room and look at them?'

'Of course. My dear, I'm more sorry than I can say. The fellow is a blackguard—a scoundrel. He should be horsewhipped for treating you like this.'

She said, 'I don't think they allow you to do things like that these days. Good night.'

Up in her room, she spread the typewritten sheets and the photographs on the bed, and looked at them until she felt that every black and white image, every sordid word was etched on her brain in acid.

She studied the address of the flat, and noticed that Clare Marshall was visiting a Harley Street gynaecologist. Was it to pay his fees that their savings had gone? It didn't seem possible. Yet the evidence was there in black and white—day and hour, chapter and verse.

Had Jason really imagined he could string her along in ignorance forever, she asked herself wretchedly. Did he truly think she was such a blind besotted fool?

The honest answer to both questions was probably 'Yes'. She'd had not the slightest idea that there was any woman in his life but herself. She found herself remembering those days at the studio, and the 'phone calls which had made her so jealous, and wondering if Clare Marshall had been among the callers.

The question she could not find an answer to was why Jason had not married Clare instead of herself. If she was a woman of independent means, as seemed likely, then what had stopped them? On purely mercenary grounds, she seemed a better bet as a wife than Laura Caswell, the poor relation of the rich Caswells.

Perhaps Uncle Martin had been right about that too, she thought unhappily. Maybe Jason had pursued her thinking she was an heiress, and had turned back to his former love in disillusion when he discovered the truth.

She wished she could cry, but she was hurting too much. How he must have been laughing at her, with all his talk of 'Laura alone'. How clever he'd been to seduce her first, then win her mind with all that idealistic garbage about 'mutual needs'. He'd never, she realised for the first time, actually said he loved her, merely implied that it was so.

'Oh God,' she whispered.

Grief was scalding her, twisting at her throat, but her eyes were dry and burning as she slid the scattered papers back into the folder, and closed it.

CHAPTER SEVEN

'So,' Bethany said. 'You went and got a divorce.'

'Not immediately. First, I went back to London. I went to the flat in Belgravia, and hung about for most of the morning. I hated myself for doing it, but somehow I had to see her in the flesh—know what I was up against.' Laura frowned and shook her head. 'It was a mistake.'

'I can imagine,' Bethany said drily. 'I suppose you ended up liking her.'

'She looked nicer than she did in the photographs—younger. I could see what would attract him—attract any man. She had a pleasant voice and a lovely smile. She was pregnant and blooming, and I sat across the road in a taxi and hated her for all of it.' Laura sighed. 'It was a silly hysterical thing to do, but I wasn't thinking very straight.'

'You spoke to her?' Bethany's eyebrows climbed to her hairline, and Laura smiled reluctantly.

'No, I didn't go that far. But she stopped to talk to some people—neighbours, I think and I could hear what she was saying. They called her Mrs Wingard, and I remember thinking that hadn't been on the detective's report. It made me very angry and so it was possible to do what I had to do next.' She paused. 'I went across London to see Jason.'

He had just been coming out of the studio. When he saw her his face lit up with surprise, and what she would have sworn was delight.

He said, 'I was going to 'phone tonight and tell your uncle I wanted my wife back. Come up to the studio, I have something to show you.'

She followed him up the stairs. 'And I have something to say to you.'

'Say it then,' he threw casually over his shoulders. 'I'll make the coffee.'

'I don't want any coffee.' The note in her voice made him turn and study her, his brows drawing together in a frown.

He said, 'You look like death. Your few days in the country don't seem to have done a great deal of good.'

'On the contrary, I see all kinds of things in a completely new light.' She made herself look him in the face. 'Jason—tell me one thing. The money from our account, did you give it to Clare Marshall and her child—her children?'

She stood, watching the colour drain out of his face at her words. She realised she'd been praying for some kind of miracle—a denial—a complete vindication. She'd been praying for the impossible.

'Someone,' he said after a long, terrible silence, 'appears to have been busy. Let me guess. Can it have been kindly Uncle Martin?'

'Does it matter? It's true, isn't it? You've been taking my paltry allowance and giving it to your mistress to support her and her child. You were letting us scratch round for a deposit on a house while she was living like a queen. You were sleeping with her. My God.' Her voice cracked. 'No wonder you didn't really want my baby. Why should you when you had a ready-made family already?'

He was white and there was a muscle jumping dangerously at his temple. He said, 'I'm warning you, Laura. Stop right there. Don't say another word.'

'You mean—turn the other cheek? Pretend it's never happened? Play the pathetic wife, grateful for small mercies?'

'No,' he exploded. 'That isn't what I mean at all.

Laura—for God's sake—trust me, please. If I could explain to you, I would.'

'Oh, I'm sure of that.' She gave a mirthless laugh. 'You have convincing explanations for everything, no doubt. But I don't want to hear any more lies, any more deception. You've been found out, Jason. Don't make things worse by inventing lame excuses.'

There was another agonising silence, then he said very quietly, 'Then there's nothing more to be said.' His eyes were colder than ice, harder than steel. It made her shiver just to look at them.

She said, 'You didn't cover your tracks very well.'

'No,' he said with a slight snarl. 'But then I didn't bargain for the intervention of your uncle. Stupid of me.'

'It isn't his fault. You can't blame him. He was simply thinking of me.' She moved restively. 'Why did you marry me, Jason?'

His mouth twisted in bitter cynicism. His glance swept her from head to foot. He said, 'You have all the answers, darling. Work it out for yourself.'

She gave a little broken sigh, and turned away. She reached the door, her hand tugging at the latch which had stuck as it sometimes did. Jason's hand descended on her shoulder, swinging her round violently to face him.

Half under his breath he said, 'To hell with this. You're going nowhere.'

He carried her to the dais, and she fought him every inch of the way.'

'Don't touch me,' she sobbed. 'Don't dare to . . .'

He said between his teeth, 'Try and stop me.'

She couldn't, of course. He was too strong and too determined, inflicting himself upon her without tenderness, or any of the subtly erotic preliminaries she had grown accustomed to. Her body was attuned to lovemaking, not the satisfaction of anger and lust, and she suffered accordingly.

When it was over, he rolled away from her and lay motionless, his head buried on his folded arms.

She sat up stiffly, straightening the clothing he'd disordered. Her body ached, and she felt a million years old.

As she got to her feet, she was half afraid he would stop her, draw her down to him again. As he moved and sat up, she was cold with fright, her eyes blank with misery as they met his.

His face was ravaged—for a moment she wondered dazedly whether he might have been crying, but she knew it was impossible.

He said hoarsely, 'So—I've lost you, thanks to your uncle. I'll make him pay for this—for all of it.'

The words seemed to pursue her down the stairs, and into the street outside. For a moment, she thought he was following her, and half-turned, but the pavement behind her was deserted. Once again, she was alone.

There was a long silence, then she looked at Bethany. 'Now you know it all.'

'Yes.' Bethany sat, her chin resting reflectively on her hand. 'As far as anyone can, of course. And there are still a hell of a lot of things still unanswered. Hasn't that occurred to you?'

Laura shrugged. 'Yes—but there seemed no point in pursuing any of them. They made no basic difference. They couldn't make Clare Marshall and her children disappear.'

'And you say she's here?'

Laura nodded. 'In the flesh. She was looking in the estate agent's opposite.'

'You couldn't have been mistaken?' Bethany bit her lip. 'After all, it's been a long time.'

'If it was a hundred years, I'd know her again.' Laura swung her legs to the floor. 'I must be going. I've pestered you quite long enough . . .'

'Idiot,' Bethany said calmly. 'Has he married her, do you suppose?'

Laura shook her head. 'He told Celia that he had no wife, but I can't believe that her being here is simply a coincidence.'

'Neither can I.' Bethany frowned. 'But you have to admit that their relationship is one of the most puzzling aspects of the entire story. Why the hell have they never married? They have a long-standing liaison—children, and he can afford now to keep her in the manner to which she's accustomed. So why do they hesitate?'

Laura said flatly, 'Perhaps she knows him too well—knows that for him marriage would never work with any woman.'

'A lousy husband, but a good father?' Bethany grimaced. 'That doesn't make a whole lot of sense.' She paused. 'Have you never asked yourself why your uncle chose that particular moment to tell you what he'd found out? I mean—you were getting over a miscarriage—in a low state, and he dumps all that on you. Why didn't he confront Jason himself instead?'

Laura said slowly, 'I suppose—because he disliked him too much.'

'He seemed positively paranoid about him from day one,' Bethany commented acidly. 'How has he reacted to the fact that he's back?'

'He's—accepted it.' Laura shrugged. 'He had no other choice. Jason isn't a nobody any more, whatever his morals. He can put a lucrative contract in Uncle Martin's way.'

'And this is why he's reappeared—to do your uncle a favour?' Bethany stared at her. 'Oh come on, Laura. You don't believe that.'

'No, I don't, and I've tried to warn Uncle Martin, but he doesn't want to know.'

Bethany gave her a caustic look. 'I wouldn't worry

too much about your uncle. I imagine he can look out for himself. It's you that I'm concerned about.'

'Don't be—please.' Laura stood up. 'You have quite enough to deal with here. It's been a relief to talk about it, Beth, and I'm truly grateful, but it's not your problem. I'll find a way out somehow.'

'And your cousin Celia? How are you going to cope with that aspect of the situation?' Bethany shook her head. 'I'm amazed that your uncle has allowed Jason Wingard within a thousand miles of any of his family, business deal or no business deal. Unless he's less concerned about his daughter than he was about you, of course.'

Laura smiled tautly. 'No—but as I explained, the situation has changed. Jason is a wealthy man in his own right now. Uncle Martin may not like him, but one of his main objections doesn't exist any more.'

'In other words, just because he's rich—all is forgiven?' Bethany sounded stupified. 'That's the most cynical thing I've ever heard.'

'Yes.' Laura bit her lip. 'The last twenty-four hours haven't been the easiest of my life.'

'I can imagine,' Bethany muttered. She put a hand on Laura's arm, and gave it a comforting squeeze. 'If you ever feel you have to run, then there's always a bolthole here. We have a spare room, and even a camp bed, and if bookings continue at their present rate, Mike's going to need help with the cooking.'

Tears pricked at Laura's eyes. 'Oh, Beth, that's so good of you. I'm only sorry our reunion has been so downbeat,' she added with a little shaky laugh.

'Don't worry about it. From here, the only way is up.' Bethany rose briskly. 'And now I'm going to make some more coffee. I think we both need it.'

Laura felt infinitely more cheerful as she emerged into the street some half-hour later. Talking to Bethany like that, pouring out everything that had happened had been a strange experience, but it had helped her to get things into perspective, made her consider them in a new light after all this time.

For so long, she had tried not to think about it, had tried to block that unhappy time in her mind as if it had never existed. But it hadn't worked, and now she knew why. Bethany was quite right—there were too many unanswered questions as she might have realised at the time, if she hadn't been at such a low ebb, physically and mentally.

She had also been made to realise unwillingly that whatever Jason had done, whatever harm and misery he had caused, his power over her was as strong as ever.

Perhaps that was her own fault, she thought sombrely. Perhaps she was the kind of woman who only loved once in her life, and remained faithful to that love, no matter how big a bastard the man in her life turned out to be.

And perhaps Jason was the kind of man who was able to inspire that kind of fidelity, she told herelf unhappily. The fact that Clare Marshall was still in his orbit seemed to indicate that.

She found herself wondering about the other woman, wondering how much she had suffered when Jason had failed to return the previous night. Or was she so used to his philandering that it no longer made any difference?

Two of us wanting him, she thought, and he isn't worth it. If it wasn't so sad, it would almost be funny.

A voice close beside her said, 'Laura' and she turned quickly to see Alan's sheepish face.

He looked so woebegone that it drew a smile from her. 'How's the hangover?'

'Improving,' he said pallidly. 'Laura, I can't apologise enough. God, I'm so sorry. I'm going to sign the pledge, I swear it. I know that I've never had a good head for alcohol, but I've never made such an utter fool of myself before.'

She said lightly, 'Well, don't worry about it. I'm afraid your car has collected a ticket.'

'Yes.' He produced it from his pocket and gave it a sour look. 'I suppose I'd better go and get it sorted out.' He hesitated. 'I only hope I haven't put you off me for life.'

Laura hesitated too. It occurred to her that it might be kinder to tell Alan here and now that there was no room for him in her life, and that she had been wrong if she'd ever encouraged him to think differently. The hopeful note in his voice made her feel guilty.

She said, 'Alan . . .' and saw over his shoulder Jason's tall figure approaching down Burngate.

The breath caught in her throat, then she transferred her gaze to Alan, smiling at him brilliantly. She said, 'Don't be silly. Of course I haven't been put off,' and leaned forward, kissing him swiftly on the cheek.

For a moment, he looked as dazed as if she'd hit him with a brick—it was the first time she'd volunteered any kind of caress—then his smile splintered into equal parts of surprise and gratification.

He said eagerly, 'Then what about tonight? There's a good folk group playing at the Four Winds. If I picked you up around seven?'

'It sounds marvellous,' Laura said with no truth whatever.

Jason said silkily, 'Good morning. I hope I'm not interrupting an assignation.'

Alan turned to him. 'Oh hello. Look I have to apologise to you as well for last night.'

Jason shrugged. 'It happens.' He sounded faintly bored. 'Next time don't mix your drinks.'

'I won't,' Alan agreed rather mournfully. 'And I've got a parking ticket. I'm going to remember last night for a long time.'

Jason said softly, 'I'm sure all of us will,' and despite

anything she could do, Laura felt dull colour rise in her face under his mocking glance.

She said swiftly, 'Alan, if you're going to pay that ticket, I'll walk part of the way with you . . .'

'Must you?' Jason's hand descended on her arm, detaining her. He smiled faintly down into her outraged face. 'I was hoping perhaps you could spare me an hour or two.'

'I fail to see why.' Laura shook herself free, glaring at him.

'And I'm about to explain.' He was openly amused now, and Alan was regarding them both with obvious bemusement. 'I'm house hunting locally, and I need someone who knows the area to give me some guidance.'

Laura felt stunned. She said, 'House hunting—you?' Her voice was frankly incredulous. 'You're coming to live here?'

He nodded. 'Part of the office complex we're about to build will incorporate Tristans' new headquarters. We've been thinking for some time that we need to move nearer to London, and I can hardly expect my staff to move if I don't set the example myself.'

She didn't know what to say. Her brain was whirling. From what seemed a great distance, she heard Alan say, 'That's fantastic. Just what this place needs—new industry—new blood. And it's a buyer's market in the property world just now. What size of place were you considering?'

Jason shrugged. 'I haven't any firm ideas. As well as myself, I need accommodation for my housekeeper and her two children—room for entertaining, naturally, and space for guests, and my mother perhaps.'

Alan said rather blankly, 'You'll need a mansion. That's a pretty formidable list.'

'But not, I hope, an impossible one,' Jason said. He glanced at Laura who stood motionless, her pale face concealing the welter of emotion inside her. 'What do you think?'

She said in a colourless voice. 'I'm sure any of the local agents will greet you with open arms. You really don't need any assistance.'

'Oh, but I do,' he said softly. 'The—er—woman's touch.'

She bit her lip. 'Your housekeeper could supply that.' She paused abruptly, remembering the glimpse of Clare Marshall earlier, looking in an estate agents' window.

'She'll be consulted naturally before any final decision, but she has no local knowledge.' Jason's tone was level. 'I don't want to find that I'm living under the flightpath for some airfield, or downwind of the piggeries.'

'Well, you couldn't find a better guide than Laura,' Alan assured him heartily. 'She's lived here all her life, after all, and that has to be a recommendation.' He smiled at her. 'I'll leave you both to it.' He lowered his voice almost conspiratorially. 'See you tonight.'

She was aware of a cowardly impulse to grab his sleeve and say, 'Don't go,' but instead she stood and watched him walk away.

Jason said softly, 'He's dull, Laura. Why do you tolerate him?'

'Because he's a decent human being,' she said. 'Not that decency is a quality you could be expected to appreciate.'

His brows rose. 'You're very waspish this morning, darling. Didn't you sleep last night?'

She said stonily, 'The storm woke me.'

'They always did,' he said, 'if you remember. But in those days I had an excellent remedy.'

There was sudden laughter in his voice, sensual reminiscence in his eyes as he watched her, and this time she blushed hotly and deeply as she remembered the times she had woken, frightened by thunder, in his arms, and exactly how he had comforted her.

She said icily, 'Was that what you were doing for Celia?'

'Celia?' he frowned questioningly.

'Oh, don't bother to lie.' The words tumbled over themselves. 'I'm not the naïve fool I was when you married me. And it's no concern of mine anyway what you do, or who you do it with. But I wouldn't let Uncle Martin find out. He might forget that you're an important customer and remember all the reasons he has not to like you.'

'I doubt it.' His mouth curled. 'You may think you know your uncle, Laura, but I'm telling you that to him money talks—in fact I'd say it's probably the only voice he hears.'

She glared at him. 'That's a foul thing to say.'

'It happens to be the truth. It was money that prompted him to have me removed from your life. Surely you've realised that by this time?'

'It was concern for me, and repugnance for the kind of man you are,' Laura said fiercely. 'Or are you trying to say that if Uncle Martin had realised you were the heir to Tristan Construction, he would have concealed what he'd discovered about your—liaison.'

'No,' he said drily. 'He can be acquitted of that. Although I daresay it might have given him food for thought.'

'Well, you have no right to criticise him.' She flung up her chin. 'Heaven knows you haven't changed. Except that you've obviously been reconciled with your parents. Did I hear you say your mother is to share your—menage? She must be a very broad-minded woman.'

'You think so?' he said. 'It's a lesson you could profit from yourself, darling. Unless you propose to throw in your lot with the boyfriend. Apart from a potential drink problem, he shouldn't cause you too many anxious moments.'

She shrugged. 'I think I used up my quota while we were married. I'm due for some peace.'

'Don't you mean boredom?' The grey eyes held hers, glinting.

'Perhaps I do.' She took a deep breath. 'But anything, Jason—anything would be preferable to the kind of misery you made me suffer. I hoped I'd never have to see you again.'

His eyes narrowed. 'Then you're going to be disappointed. I'm here—and I'm here to stay.' His voice deepened making the words sound like a threat.

Laura threw her head back. 'But why here—of all the places in the Home Counties?'

'I have my reasons.' His face hardened.

'Devious ones, no doubt,' she said bitterly. 'If I was my uncle, I wouldn't trust you one inch.'

'Shrewd of you, darling,' he said icily. 'You know, you're wasted as a cook. You should be in the Caswell board room, dragging them back from the brink.'

'Before you push them over?' she shot at him, and saw him stiffen. 'Before they plunge into investment in the new fibre which you profess to be so interested in? How deep a hole do you want Caswells to dig for themselves, before you pull out—tell them you've changed your mind and that the contracts will go elsewhere?'

There was a brief electric silence, then he said softly, 'Just wait and see, darling. Wait and see.'

She stood and watched him walk away from her, down Burngate, and out of sight.

The folk club, held in the cellar of a large country inn, was crowded, hot and smoky, and even before the first half of the programme had come to an end, Laura had the beginnings of a headache.

She had spent the afternoon walking, crossing fields and woodland with none of her usual awareness of their beauty, trying desperately to decide what to do for the best.

Leaving her uncle's house seemed a priority, but where was she to go? Not even the bolthole suggested by Bethany could be considered as a refuge any more. She needed to get right away.

There were jobs, she told herself over and over again. Good cooks were always in demand. She could answer advertisements, go for interviews. Something suitable would present itself.

She'd returned home for dinner to a distinctly querulous atmosphere. Uncle Martin had come back from the works, annoyed because the instant decision he'd been hoping for from Tristan Construction was clearly not forthcoming.

'I 'phoned that fellow Leng, but he was simply evasive,' he grumbled. 'Couldn't seem to give me any idea at all, except that they had other firms to see.'

He continued in a similar vein for the whole of the meal, apparently oblivious to the fact there was little response from either his daughter or his niece.

Celia, Laura thought almost pityingly, was clearly on edge, listening for the sound of a car, or the telephone.

When at last the 'phone did ring, during the dessert course, her eyes turned with painful eagerness to the door, and when Mrs Fraser put her head round the door and announced, 'It's for you, Miss Celia. Shall I tell him you're still having dinner?' Celia shot to her feet.

'No, I'll take it.'

She was back almost at once, her face sulky as she resumed her chair. It had not been the call she was waiting for.

Oh Celia, Laura said under her breath, are you so heavily involved already—after only one night?

'Who was that, my dear?' Uncle Martin asked.

Celia shrugged petulantly. 'Only Peter Curzon—wanting me to go out for a drink tonight.'

'Nice boy, Peter.' Uncle Martin nodded paternal approval.

Celia's lip curled. 'Exactly, Daddy. Hopelessly immature. I told him I was busy.'

But she was still waiting restlessly, when Laura came downstairs changed into a casual shirtwaister dress, and carrying a light wool shawl over her arm.

'Where are you going?' It sounded like the start of an inquisition, and Laura sighed soundlessly.

'Out with Alan,' she returned briefly.

'You must be a glutton for punishment, sweetie.' Celia gave her a malicious smile. 'I'd keep him off the booze if I were you. There won't be anyone around tonight to come to the rescue.'

As soon as Laura heard the car, she went out to meet Alan. She had no intention of exposing him to Celia's ideas of hospitality again. But Alan showed no signs of wishing to delay their departure.

'I should have arranged to pick you up earlier,' he said starting the engine. 'It's the Wessex Revellers tonight, and they're always popular. We'll be lucky to get a decent table.'

And if we're really lucky, Laura thought grimly as they drove through the lanes, there'll be no tables left at all.

Alan was enthusiastic and knowledgeable about folk music, and at any other time, Laura might have found an evening at the Four Winds in his company an enjoyable event. But tonight she was far too preoccupied with her problems to enter into the spirit of the event, and she felt guiltily that she was being unfair to Alan. It would have been more honest to do as Celia had done, and made some excuse, she told herself.

Alan came back from the bar with two lagers. He

handed her one, and lifted the other towards her in a toast, with a self-conscious grimace. 'To us.'

There is no 'us', she thought with a sudden great sadness. There never can be, and I should tell you so before you say something or do something to commit yourself any further.

I'll tell him I'm going away, she decided, welcoming the cool lager into her dry throat. I'll make it sound very casual as if it's something that's been on the cards for a long time, as if I never regarded our relationship as any more than friendship. That's all I can do, and I only hope it's enough to act as a face-saver for him.

And once she'd told him, she would have to do something, commit herself to some positive course of action, instead of sitting round like a helpless puppet letting fate deal some grotesque jerk at her strings.

Tomorrow, she thought. I'll start tomorrow. She leaned back in her chair, feeling as if she'd won some victory, and looked up to see, across the haze of the smoke-filled room, Jason's face. Watching her.

She thought, 'I'm imagining things. He can't be there. I'm in such a state I'm hallucinating. Inventing him.'

Then the crowd shifted and she saw the girl with him. Saw the smooth dark hair, the face eager and warm with laughter lifted to his.

It was the first time she'd ever seen them together in the flesh, and the pain of it stunned her.

She found herself thinking mechanically, 'So that's why Celia didn't get her call—because he'd decided to pay some attention to his first love.'

Incredulously she watched as they both rose from their seats. Her hands gripped the edge of the table so tightly that her knuckles turned white. He was—bringing her over.

'Good evening.' The dark face was enigmatic, the eyes cool and watchful as he greeted them. Alan was rising, looking surprised. Laura felt frozen to the spot. Under her lashes, she stole a look at Clare Marshall, wondering how she was feeling, how she was responding to Jason's latest cruelty. She had to be suffering too, as shocked and embarrassed at this enforced confrontation as Laura was herself.

If so, she was concealing it well. She seemed at ease, smiling, her face friendly and interested.

Jason said silkily, 'I don't think you two have met. Laura, this is Clare Marshall. Clare, this is Laura Caswell.' He paused. 'My ex-wife,' he added softly.

Laura heard Alan's intake of breath, felt his eyes on her, trying to make sense of what he had just heard.

There was no guilt or embarrassment in Clare Marshall's face, only a certain wryness in her smile. She said, 'I'd rather guessed that already. How do you do, Laura?'

She held out her hand, and Laura took it like an automaton, stammering the conventional greeting in reply.

There was a deafening silence, then Laura said jerkily, 'Do you like—this kind of music—Miss Marshall?'

'It's a long time since I saw a live performance. Not since my student days, in fact, but I enjoy it—yes.' Clare Marshall said. 'And Jason insisted I had to hear the Wessex Revellers.' She shrugged. 'I have domestic commitments, so I don't get out much in the evenings.'

Laura said woodenly, 'That's a shame. Well—I hope you enjoy the rest of the concert.'

It was more than she was going to do, if the expression on Alan's face was anything to go by. She'd watched it change from sheer incredulity to jealous indignation, and although he was probably not aware of all the undercurrents seething below the surface of the exchange, he was clearly going to ask questions.

'Which is just about to begin,' Jason said smoothly.

'We'd better get back to our seats.' His smile flicked at Laura. 'I'll be seeing you.'

Alan said furiously, 'What the hell did he mean—ex-wife? What . . .?'

'Later, please.' Laura tugged imploring at his sweater sleeve, aware of curious glances from neighbouring tables. The lights were going down, the applause to greet the Wessex Revellers was swelling enthusiastically. For a moment, she thought he was going to walk out, then he subsided back into his chair, his face sullen.

It hadn't been the night of her life, up to that moment, but now it was totally in ruins, and Jason had done it quite deliberately. But for what motive? That was the question which battered at her mind. To punish her for the things she had said to him earlier? Perhaps—but why involve his mistress, force her into an awkward confrontation that she couldn't have wanted, no matter how skilfully she'd covered up? Clare Marshall wasn't some cowed, submissive little creature, so why did she allow herself to be used like that?

Because she loves him, Laura told herself painfully. Because however strange their relationship, however unsatisfactory it might seem to an outsider, it must provide everything Clare Marshall needs, or she would not still be with him, and with him in an apparently menial position. Fleetingly, Laura wondered what had happened to the expensive flat.

The music washed over her, unheard. Mechanically, she joined in the applause at the end of each song, and was eventually aroused by the jovial whistling and stamping going on around her to the realisation that the performance was over.

'Let's go,' Alan said shortly, and got up.

Laura hung back. 'There are going to be encores.'

'I've had enough,' he muttered. 'We have to talk.' He took her hand, pulling her to her feet. 'Come on.'

He walked across the car park so fast that she almost had to run to keep up with him, and she could feel her own temper rising.

She said abruptly, 'It might be better if I got a taxi.'

He glared at her. 'I think you owe me an explanation.'

'Perhaps,' she said shortly. 'But this may not be the ideal time.'

He was holding the car door open for her. Other people were beginning to emerge into the car park, and she didn't want a scene, so, biting her lip, she got into the car.

She had expected he would take her home, but after they had been driving for a few moments, she realised he was on his way to the cottage.

She said, 'Alan, we can't talk tonight. I'm tired and . . .'

'And I'm supposed to fall into line and be a gentleman, and pretend it doesn't matter.' He spoke jeeringly, his face flushed, 'Well, it does damned well matter—Miss Caswell,' he added with extra emphasis. 'You've made a bloody fool of me.'

'I fail to see how.' Laura shook her head.

With an impatient exclamation, he pulled the wheel over and brought the car to a stop on the roadside verge.

'It never occurred to you that the fact you've been married before might be of interest to me?' he demanded.

She sighed. 'I suppose I would have told you—if our relationship had warranted it. But as things are . . .'

'As things are,' he repeated savagely. 'Didn't it also occur to you that the reason I've allowed you to keep me at a distance, agreed to play it cool is because I thought you were an inexperienced girl—not a divorcee?'

He made it sound as if she was Lucrezia Borgia, and she knew a traitorous desire to giggle, but she restrained it because he was a man with a grievance, and consequently short on humour.

She said, 'I'm sorry. I didn't intend to deceive you about my—my marital status. It's simply a subject I've always preferred not to discuss—with anyone.'

'How long were you married?' He stared through the windscreen.

'About a year. We divorced by consent at the earliest legal opportunity,' she said levelly. 'Is there anything else you need to know?'

'Yes.' He turned and gave her an insolent look. 'I'd like to know why the marriage—broke down as they put it these days. Did you freeze him off, like you've tried to freeze me? I thought you were just shy, but perhaps it goes deeper than that. Perhaps you're frigid. Let's see shall we?'

He lunged across the confined space of the car, dragging her into his arms, clamping his mouth to hers without finesse.

Any fleeting sympathy she might have had for his confusion vanished instantly, and she tried to pull away, disgust rising in her as his hand hooked into the neckline of her dress.

She heard a ripping sound, felt the buttons tear loose. He lifted his head and stared at her, his eyes fixed greedily on her breasts, barely concealed by the delicate lace cups of her bra. He said hoarsely, 'I held back because I thought you were a virgin. But you're not, Laura. You've been married to a man like Wingard, so you know what it's all about.' His tone slurred. 'You must want it sometimes—like I've been wanting you . . .'

He was reaching for her again. With a kind of desperation, she hit him in the face as hard as she could with her clenched fist.

He gave an agonised yelp, and slumped back into the driving seat, covering his face with his hands. With horrified fascination, Laura saw blood begin to seep through his fingers and realised she must have caught him on the nose.

Again she felt that hysterical laughter welling up inside her. She opened her bag hastily. 'Here—I've got some tissues.'

He mumbled, 'Bitch,' but he took the tissues, pressing them to his nose.

She waited for a few moments, then said, 'Do you want me to drive?'

He glared at her over the tissues. 'No—just get out of my sight.'

For a moment, she was taken aback. The last thing she was expecting was to be stranded miles from home with a torn dress, but this was clearly what he intended, his sense of grievance outweighing all other considerations.

She said, 'I'm sorry it had to turn out like this.' Her voice sounded lame. Nothing that had happened to her seemed to have any basis in reality, although she supposed her dress gaping open to the waist was real enough.

She hugged her shawl round her and watched him drive away, fumbling with gears and tissues, then began to walk slowly back the way she had come.

She'd covered about half a mile when she heard the sound of a car engine behind her, and she stepped on to the verge, looking back over her shoulder, hoping against hope that Alan might have come to his senses and be looking for her.

But it wasn't the small comfortable shape of the Mini which came round the corner, transfixing her in its headlights like a frightened moth. It was an altogether more opulent vehicle and it was stopping, she realised with sudden panic, realising all the dangers of her situation.

She turned precipitately to hurry away, but one of

her heels sank into the earth of the verge, softened by the previous night's rain and she stumbled almost on to her knees.

She struggled up, hearing the approaching footsteps. Even before his hands pulled her to her feet, she knew who it was.

Even before she heard his voice, drawling, mocking— 'Running away again, Laura? Don't you know by this time that there's nowhere—nowhere you can run to?'

CHAPTER EIGHT

ALL the strength, the resistance seemed to have drained out of her. She let him put her into the front passenger seat of the Jaguar.

He said, as if anticipating the question he knew she wouldn't ask aloud, 'Clare's gone back to the hotel. One of the chambermaids is baby-sitting but naturally, she's anxious.'

'Naturally.' Her voice sounded brittle. 'So you decided you'd go for a moonlight drive in the lanes.'

'No,' he said. 'I saw your hasty departure, and it occurred to me that he might turn nasty, so I thought I'd drive over to his cottage and see if you were there.'

'Thoughtful of you,' she said bitterly. 'What a pity the possibility of his adverse reaction didn't—occur to you earlier, before you dropped your bombshell.'

'You intended to keep our marriage as your little secret did you?' he gibed. 'Were you going to wait till the honeymoon to break the news that he'd bought secondhand goods?'

'You're vile.'

'And he, of course, has behaved like a knight in shining armour. That's why he let you take the long walk home. Or did you think that he'd be content to go on adoring you from afar?'

'I didn't think of it at all,' she confessed bleakly. 'We'd never had that kind of relationship.'

'By your wish, not his, I'm sure.' His mouth twisted. 'Couldn't you see the way the poor devil was looking at you?'

She shook her head, unable to find words.

'You can hardly blame him,' he continued harshly.

'It's that special quality you possess, Laura. I've mentioned it before—that air of solitariness and self-containment. Small wonder if he thought of you as the sleeping princess, and dreamed of the kiss that would waken you. It must have been gall and wormwood to know that another man had got you into bed first.'

She winced. 'Don't.' She put her hands over her ears, and the shawl fell open.

She saw his swift downward glance and remembered too late.

He said too softly, 'I think I'll knock his teeth down his throat.'

'Oh, no—please.' She put a hand on his arm, alarmed. 'There's no need. Nothing happened—really.'

'You tore your own dress——' he said derisively.

'No.' That weird laughter she'd been trying to suppress all evening came bubbling to the surface. 'But—poor Alan—he's suffered enough for one night. I—I made his nose bleed.'

She was laughing helplessly, and suddenly she was crying too, sobbing until the sting of his hand across her cheek shocked her into silence.

She whispered, 'How dare you.'

'Quite easily. You're hysterical,' he said coldly.

'And whose fault is that?' Her hands clenched into fists in her lap. 'Who—provoked every damned thing that's happened this evening—bringing that Marshall woman across to meet me.'

He said laconically, 'I thought it was time you met.'

'All part of the—civilised behaviour I've heard so much about,' she asked wildly. 'Well—she's an acquaintance I can well do without. And if you'd bothered to ask her she would probably have told you the same thing.'

'You're wrong,' he said. 'She's always wanted to meet you.'

There was a blank silence, then Laura said, 'She must be twisted.'

He shook his head, 'She's very sane and sensible. Rather too warm-hearted, perhaps,' he added after a pause.

She said, 'But you of all people should be the last one to complain about that.'

'Wrong again,' he said and there was silence.

At last, Laura said, 'May I ask you something? You—you no longer have any reason to hide things from me.'

'Ask anything you want,' Jason said, and there was an odd note in his voice.

'The quarrel with your parents,' she said. 'Was that over—Miss Marshall?'

'Yes,' he said.

'Were you working for Tristan Construction—for your father at the time?'

He nodded. 'That had always been the idea. I was the heir—the only son, so my father's shoes were waiting for me. I wanted to do an art course, but I ended up in architecture instead.'

'That's a pity.'

'It was practical,' he returned. 'At the time, I was quite prepared to continue painting as a hobby.'

'And then you met—Clare.' She bit her lip.

'We were students together. When we got our degrees she came to work at Tristans as well. The company was expanding rapidly at that time.'

'I see,' Laura said quietly.

'No more questions?' There was mockery in his tone, and something guarded too.

She shook her head. There were a million buzzing in her head, but there was no reason why he should allow her to indulge her curiosity any more. 'After all this time—it hardly matters, does it?'

'If you say so.' His voice was flat and bitter, and she

looked at him quickly. He was reaching for the ignition, his face oddly haggard. 'So I'll just drive you back to the shelter of kindly Uncle Martin. That's what you want, I presume.'

She said, 'Thank you.'

They were there almost before she knew it. He couldn't wait to be rid of her, she thought. He couldn't wait to get back to Clare, whose hold on him after all these years was as strong as ever.

As the car turned into the drive, she said suddenly, 'Why don't you marry her?'

'Because she doesn't want to be married to me,' he said. 'A thing you both obviously have in common.'

The note in his voice made her flinch. She said, 'But the children—Jason . . .'

'Are well-looked after, and financially secure.'

As I was, she thought. But that didn't stop me wanting my own, real family like other people had.

She said, 'Have you ever asked her?'

'Yes.' He switched off the engine. His hands gripped the steering wheel. 'As a matter of fact, I did once, and she turned me down. Satisfied?'

He sounded raw, and she said hurriedly, 'Oh God, I'm sorry. I shouldn't go on like this. I have no right to ask . . .'

He said with a kind of controlled violence, 'Oh, yes, my lovely Laura, you had every right. Only you never did, my darling. You never asked any of the right questions—when it mattered. Just stood there and accused me—let me know once and for all just how low you rated me—our marriage—everything.' He gave an angry laugh. 'No wonder that poor idiot lost his temper with you when he found he didn't mean anything either. You were lucky to get away with a torn dress.'

She was trembling. 'I didn't—from you.'

'No,' he said softly, 'You didn't.' He turned towards her. His hand brushed aside the edges of her dress, uncovering her. The long fingers found the tiny clasp which fastened her bra at the front and released it. His hand cupped her breast, his questioning thumb discovering the hardening nipple in a caress which made her whole body convulse in pleasure. 'At times, my once wife, revenge can be—more than sweet.' He sat back, his eyes insolently assessing the unmistakable evidence of her arousal. 'As you will discover—because I haven't finished with you. I'm going to make you sorry for every hard word you said to me.'

'Does the truth hurt so much?' Her face was burning. Her hands shook as she re-fastened her bra.

'Truth,' he said contemptuously. 'What the hell do you know about the truth? All those questions and yet you still haven't asked the one that matters.'

'I don't understand . . .'

'No—and you never did.' The grey eyes looked at her grimly. 'And now I advise you to get out of this car while you still can. Or I might turn the clock back to that day in the studio, and you wouldn't like that. Would you?'

Dry-throated, she said, 'No.'

The night air was warm, but she was shivering as she stood in the shelter of the stone porch and watched the tail-lights of the Jaguar vanish down the drive.

Because no matter how much she might try to deny it, no matter whether it was in anger or in hatred, she knew that she wanted him still, and that she always would.

It was a long time before she fell asleep that night, and the following morning she woke late and heavy-eyed.

On her way downstairs she encountered Mrs Fraser crossing the hall with a tray of used breakfast things, and received a sour look and an enquiry as to whether she wanted something to eat.

'Just orange juice and coffee will be fine.' Laura

despised herself for the placatory note she heard in her
voice, but Mrs Fraser never failed to imply by her
attitude that she was an outsider in the house, and an
unwanted inconvenience. She added levelly, 'But if it's
too much trouble, I can wait until Miss Celia comes
downstairs.'

Mrs Fraser snorted. 'Miss Celia has had her
breakfast and gone out,' she announced and vanished
towards the kitchen.

Laura glanced at her watch in amazement. Early
rising had never been among her cousin's failings, and it
was hardly ten o'clock.

To her surprise, Uncle Martin was still in the dining
room, staring frowningly into space over a cooling cup
of coffee. He roused himself sufficiently to give her
a perfunctory greeting, but his expression was still
grim.

'Is anything wrong?' Laura helped herself to orange
juice from the jug on the sideboard.

He shrugged slightly. 'The usual problems.' He
paused. 'Your ex-husband was on the telephone at
some unearthly hour.' He gave her an irritable look.
'Did you know he was planning to live in the area?'

'It—was mentioned.' Laura sat down.

'God damn him.' Her uncle relapsed into his brown
study once more, until interrupted by Mrs Fraser
arriving with a fresh coffee pot which she set in front of
Laura with a subdued thump.

He roused himself again. 'Celia's gone out with him,'
he disclosed abruptly. 'Looking at properties.'

Some of the coffee Laura was pouring spilled into the
saucer. She set the pot down on the table with more
than usual care. 'You're allowing this?' she asked.

He shrugged again. 'How can I stop her? She's her
own mistress. Oh, I know what you're thinking,' he
went on with a defensive wave of the hand. 'But the
situation is altogether different now.'

'Why?' Laura asked bitterly. 'Because Jason is now a rich man, and not the ne'er do well you thought him when we were married? Is it his money that makes the difference?'

He brought his fist down on the table. 'It's the power he wields. We need the work he can bring us, and if Celia can help clinch the contract by looking over a few houses for him, then she does it with my blessing. Besides, she can look after herself. She's not a naïve child.'

'As I was?' Laura's lip twisted unhappily. 'I don't understand you any more, Uncle Martin. The objections you had to Jason on moral grounds still hold good. His—lady, Clare Marshall, is still with him. In fact, they're going to occupy this house he's looking for together.'

He drank the rest of his coffee, and pushed his chair back. 'His morals are no longer my concern,' he said flatly.

'Not even if Celia becomes—involved?' She stared at him with utter incredulity. 'You surely don't mean to encourage . . .'

'I don't mean to encourage—or discourage.' He got to his feet. 'Celia knows what she's doing. I wish as much as you do—probably more—that this fellow Wingard had never come back into our lives, but he's here, and there's very little we can do about it. We just have to make the best of the situation.'

Laura got to her feet too, her eyes sparking with anger. 'I'm afraid I'm not prepared to do that. I think perhaps it's time I found myself another job—moved right away from here.'

On the other occasions when she'd made this suggestion, there had been an instant protest, but now he said heavily, 'Under the circumstances, that might be a solution—not of course that I wish to drive you away, Laura.' His voice roughened slightly. 'You're a good child, and I—I wish things could have been different. But I did what I thought was best. At the time it seemed there was no alternative, but now . . .' There was a long pause, then he said quietly, 'I hope one day you'll be able to forgive me, Laura.'

She watched the door close behind him, feeling utterly bewildered. These sudden changes of mood were uncharacteristic to say the least, and his attitude to Jason was confusing.

Was he now trying to say that he wished he hadn't interfered in her marriage after all? It seemed unbelievable, she thought numbly, but so was his reaction to Celia's involvement with Jason. Anger—hostility—resentment, she could have understood, but not this kind of resignation. And it was ridiculous for him to say that Celia did as she pleased. Martin Caswell was an indulgent father, but he'd acted in the past to prevent Celia from pursuing some course of action which he strongly objected to, and it was impossible that he actually favoured Celia having any kind of relationship with Jason.

He could stop it if he wanted to, she thought wretchedly, so why didn't he want to? Was it really just for the sake of a business deal, and if so, how far was he prepared to let the relationship go?

Laura shook her head. Whatever the answers were, she would not be around to find out.

Jason had said he would make her sorry, she thought bitterly, and he'd chosen the ideal method. Even the thought of him with Celia could produce an agony too deep for tears. She could not bear to watch while Celia flaunted her conquest in front of her, as she'd no doubt she would.

Perhaps she really wants him, she told herself wearily, and perhaps he wants her, and he's not just using her to torture me.

It would be comforting to think that Jason had no

idea that she still had any feeling for him, but she cherished no such illusion. She had given herself away in a dozen ways already, she knew, and to run away would be the ultimate in self-betrayal, yet what else could she do and preserve her emotional sanity?

But perhaps this time he would not follow, and she would be left alone to find some kind of peace.

Peace. She tried the word aloud, experimentally. It was soft and gentle on her tongue. A healing word for the wound she carried deep inside her.

She thought wildly. 'I'm too young to feel like this. I've still got my whole life ahead of me . . .'

A life without Jason—as bleak and empty as a desert.

Laura pushed the letter back into its envelope and slid it across the table to Bethany. 'Another "no",' she said with a sigh. 'That's four job applications and four negative replies. I might just start to develop a complex.'

Bethany grinned at her. 'Ah, but one of the negative replies was from you,' she said. 'You can't have forgotten the nursing home with hot and cold running cockroaches.'

Laura shuddered, 'No, but I'm trying to.' She tapped the envelope with her nail. 'It's a pleasant letter. She thinks I'm too young, like the others did.'

Bethany studied her through narrowed eyes. 'You need about another ten years in age, and two stone in weight. Cooks shouldn't look as if a breath of wind might blow them away. It's a bad advertisement.' She patted Laura's hand. 'But all isn't lost. You can always stay on and work here, you know that. Mike was saying yesterday that he didn't know how we were going to manage without you.'

Laura smiled. 'You've both been darlings, and you'll never know how grateful I am—but it wouldn't work. I have to get right away—somehow.'

She had been able to use the excuse of being needed at the restaurant to absent herself from the house as much as possible over the past month, so she didn't have to watch Jason and Celia there together, although she knew his visits were an almost daily event.

She knew because Celia told her so, her eyes bright with triumphant malice. Celia was enjoying herself, showing Jason off even as she showed him round the locality. She talked constantly about him when he wasn't there, describing the houses they had looked at, the meals they had shared, all the points they had in common.

And it was no consolation for Laura to suspect that Uncle Martin found Celia's carefully artless confidences as painful as she did herself.

Her uncle, she thought with compunction, was beginning to look his age. That bluff, hale look was deserting him, and there was a sallow tinge to his skin, although he denied testily that there was anything physically wrong with him.

He was worried, she knew. The Tristan name was all over town. The hoardings had gone up around the earmarked sites, and the bulldozers had moved in, but the contract with Caswells was still unsigned, even though the new fibre was in production. Caswells were being stalled, politely but inexorably. When any decision was made, they would be informed, was the invariable reply to their queries, and all Laura's early misgivings had been aroused again. But she didn't speak of them to her uncle. He had problems enough already, and she was aware that the remainder of the board were becoming restive as the days passed.

For herself, Laura found it was hardly possible to go anywhere in the town without being reminded of her ex-husband, through the company he controlled, nor was it always feasible to avoid him at the house.

There were times when she had to face him there, and

it was never easy or painless for her, yet she had to behave as if it was, aware all the time of Celia's watchful malicious gaze. She could tell herself she was managing very well. Most of the time, Jason treated her as if she was merely an acquaintance, and Laura began to feel that perhaps he had thought better of his threat, and was too involved in his building projects, and perhaps too charmed by her cousin, to bother about her any more. But then she would look up suddenly and see him watching her, like a cat with a mouse, and she would know, with heart-stopping certainty, that he hadn't finished with her yet.

If he was trying to find the best way to hurt her, then he had already succeeded beyond his wildest dreams, she thought bitterly. Simply to see his dark head bent towards Celia, to hear him laugh at one of her deliberately outrageous remarks was a punishment far worse than anything he could have deliberately devised.

And with every day which passed, it became more imperative for Laura to get away. The trouble was it had never occurred to her how difficult it might be. There were plenty of posts advertised in magazines and daily newspapers, and so far she had chosen carefully, picking those which sounded congenial at least, but she was now beginning to realise she couldn't go on being so fastidious.

One prospective employer, she was sure, had turned her down at interview because she had an unmarried son in his late twenties living with her, and regarded Laura as a threat of some kind to this happy situation. Douglas Meade was inclined to plumpness, and had a humourless face, and Laura wished there was some way of assuring his doting mother that she wouldn't have him gift-wrapped, but that of course had been impossible and instead she had to listen without comment to his mother's flurried excuses about her lack of years and experience.

She had been circumspect too about her job applications because she didn't want Celia to find out what she was doing. In ordinary circumstances, she received little mail, and a sudden heavy increase in letters for her would have attracted Celia's attention and led to the kind of questions she didn't want to answer. Whether or not her uncle knew what she was doing, Laura couldn't be sure. He didn't ask, and she didn't volunteer the information. There would be time enough, she thought, when she had a job and a new home to go to.

Now, she gave a little sigh and got up from the table. 'Well—back to the drawing board. This time I'm going to apply for everything, no matter how grotty it sounds.'

'Yuck,' Bethany said despondently. She hesitated for a moment. 'Laurie—do you really have to get a job? You told me your uncle makes you an allowance, so couldn't you just—go away for a while, get things into a fresh perspective.'

Laura smiled wrily. 'The allowance wouldn't cover that for very long,' she said. 'Not these days, anyway, and besides . . .' she paused. 'Besides, Caswells has been on the spot financially for a while, and I haven't been drawing the full amount.'

'Isn't that rather silly?' Bethany frowned a little. 'After all, you need it now and . . .'

'I need to be independent,' Laura interrupted gently. 'Which is a rather different thing, and that's why I need a job—any job, but preferably one that offers accommodation, at first anyway. I'll look at more ads and write more letters, and hope for the best.'

She had the house to herself when she arrived back with her little haul of newspapers and periodicals. She made herself a tray of tea and carried it into the drawing room where she sat, poring through the 'Situations Vacant' columns, and ringing in pencil anything that seemed remotely promising.

She was so absorbed that she didn't hear the sound of a car drawing up outside, and the first hint she received that she was no longer alone was Celia's laughing voice in the hall.

Laura swore under her breath and bundled her newspapers under one of the sofa cushions. It made the cushion lop-sided and she was smoothing it hastily when the drawing room door opened and her cousin walked in, with Jason just behind her.

Laura straightened aware that the colour had deepened in her face, and hoping that it could be explained by the fact that she'd been stooping.

Celia's brows lifted. 'I didn't expect to find you here. I thought you'd be laying tables at your little café, or whatever it is you do there.'

'I make puddings,' Laura returned pleasantly. 'And tonight I shall serve them, but in the meantime I'll go up to my room.'

Jason said coolly, 'Please don't go on my account,' and the irony of that seemed to grip her by the throat.

Without looking at him, she said, 'I'm not. I'm going to have a rest before I change. It's always hectic at the restaurant on Friday evenings.'

On her way upstairs, she wished she hadn't panicked over her newspapers. If she'd just hung on to them and left the room carrying them, Celia would probably have thought nothing of it, but for Laura to have started searching around under sofa cushions would have aroused all her curiosity, so she'd been forced to leave them where they were until later.

She took a leisurely bath, then lay down on her bed, making herself relax quite deliberately, trying to shut her ears to the small noises in the house, trying not to wonder whether Celia was in Jason's arms. Later, she heard Mrs Fraser return from her shopping expedition, and later still the sound of her uncle's car.

She dressed reluctantly and went downstairs. The

drawing room door stood open and she could see the room was empty, and also that it had been tidied for the evening in Mrs Fraser's usual impeccable manner. Tidied rather too well, Laura decided ruefully, when she lifted the cushion and found her papers gone.

'Looking for something?'

Laura jumped, and turned swiftly to find Jason framed in the french windows, watching her.

She bit her lip. 'N-no. Just—tidying up.'

His brows rose. 'I thought your dragon lady did that. It was to escape from her ministrations that I went into the garden.'

She said, 'I thought you'd gone' and coloured, wishing the words unspoken.

He sent her a mocking glance. 'Sorry to disappoint you. Your cousin has invited me to stay for dinner. We have something to celebrate.'

Laura's mouth was as dry as a bone. 'Really?' Her tone suggested a total lack of interest. 'If you'll excuse me, I'll see if Mrs Fraser needs a hand with anything.'

'I'm sure she doesn't.' He walked forward into the room. 'She seems terrifyingly efficient to me.' He stopped, resting his hands lightly on his hips and looked at her, 'Don't you want to hear my good news?'

Cat and mouse again. She stared back, her eyes flashing with resentment. 'Not particularly. Nothing you do concerns me anymore.'

He said softly, 'I can think of a number of things I could do which would concern you very deeply, my darling, and if we weren't likely to be interrupted at any moment, I might be tempted to demonstrate.'

Her colour deepened hectically, and she took a hasty step backwards. 'Don't you—dare . . .'

'Then don't you be provocative,' he came back at her sharply. 'Don't you ever learn?'

She shrugged. 'It seems not. Well—tell me your news, if it's so important.'

'It's important to me,' he said. 'I've bought a house at last.'

She'd been so sure he was going to tell her that he and Celia were engaged, that she felt almost sick with relief. She moistened her lips with the tip of her tongue. 'At last? It hasn't been that arduous, surely? You've only been house-hunting for about a month—and—and you've had Celia to help you.'

'I have indeed,' he agreed. 'She's been indispensable, although I'm afraid she's a little disappointed over my final choice. She wanted me to pick Hartley Grange, but instead I've signed the contract for Mill Cottage.'

Laura stared at him, her eyes widening. She knew the house, of course. It was a charming, old-world place, near the river. No-one knew if a miller had ever actually lived there, but the ruins of the mill itself were not far away. The house had been empty for some months after one of the elderly sisters who had lived there had died, and the other had elected to move to a comfortable private hotel for company. It was spacious enough, she thought, but it was secluded with a pretty walled garden at the rear, and the last place on earth she could imagine Jason choosing.

At last she said, 'I imagine it will need quite a lot doing to it?'

'I've had a survey done. There's a little damp which can be speedily rectified. The rest is simply a matter of up-dating things like the kitchen and bathrooms and that won't take long.'

'Naturally,' she said lightly. 'No sooner said than done. Hartley Grange, of course, has had everything done already—including a swimming pool and tennis courts. No wonder Celia is disappointed. I hope you haven't made too hasty a choice.'

He shook his head, a faint smile playing about his lips. 'No. I know what I want, and when I see it, I take it—as you, of all people, should know.'

She flushed again. In a low voice, she said, 'Don't . . .'

'I'll do what I damned well please.' His voice held suppressed violence. His hands reached and gripped her by the shoulders. He felt her flinch, and his smile deepened cruelly. 'Frightened, sweet wife? So you should be. Or did you think I'd relented—decided to forgive and forget?'

She said quietly, 'No. I don't think either of us can do that. But it doesn't solve anything—anything.' Her voice broke on the last word.

Jason's hands tightened. He said, 'But there is a solution. And you know it.' He bent, and his mouth took hers. For a moment she was still, then her trembling lips parted and her body yielded against his. His kiss deepened instantly, and his hands released their punishing grip on her shoulders to slide sensuously down the slender lines of her body to the swell of her hips, and then up again to her breasts, his fingers outlining her nipples through the soft fabric of her dress.

When at last he lifted his head, his breathing was hurried and his eyes glittered with a light which filled her with aching remembrance.

He said huskily, 'This isn't enough for either of us. I want you, Laura. Come to me.'

The urgency in his voice was matched by the clamour in her own flesh. Her throbbing pulses, the sensual quiver along her nerve endings signalled the surrender of her body, but already her mind was sounding alarms.

Because he'd said 'Come to me' not 'Come back to me' and in one small word there was spelled a whole world of difference.

She stepped away, pressing her hands against her flushed cheeks. Her voice was almost inaudible. 'No.'

'Laura.' He turned her to face him, his eyes ravaging her face. 'What the hell is this?'

She was shivering suddenly. It would be so easy to go into his arms, to give him everything he wanted, to take everything that she had ever needed. So easy, and yet so impossible, because down that road lay humiliation and disillusion as she already learned to her bitter cost.

She wrapped her arms round her body, and faced him, her chin lifted defiantly. 'I've never cared for crowds,' she said, coolly and distinctly. 'I'm not joining your harem again, Jason, now or ever. When I have a man, I need to know that, as long as it lasts, he belongs to me, totally and exclusively, and you don't fit into that category.'

He was very still for a long moment, then he laughed—a harsh ugly sound in the silence of the sunlit room.

'And do you find many of these paragons, darling?' He asked with bitter cynicism. 'If your reluctant chauffeur of the other night is a fair example, then it's little wonder that you turn to fire each time I touch you.'

She winced under the sting of his words, but managed to shrug. 'Think whatever you want. But it doesn't mean I'll ever be content with the crumbs from your table—the odd moments you have left over from your other women.' She paused. 'I assume Miss Marshall will be sharing your new home.'

'Your assumption is correct.' His eyes were granite hard as they watched her.

She said, 'Does—does my cousin know this?'

'Perhaps.' His voice was dry. 'I haven't told her, but she has her own methods of gathering information.'

'You don't think—you should tell her?'

'When the time is ripe. Not before.' His mouth twisted sardonically. 'For someone who's no longer concerned in my affairs, you seem to be taking an extraordinary interest. But you needn't fear for Celia. She's more than capable of taking care of herself.'

'I don't want to see her hurt.' She spoke intensely. 'I don't want to see any of my family hurt.'

'How compassionate,' he said. 'Why did you never extend the same clemency to me, Laura. I was your family once. Who knows? I may even be part of it again one day,' he added cynically.

'When you marry Celia?' She was aware her breathing had quickened. 'My uncle would never allow it.'

'Your uncle wouldn't be consulted,' he said insolently. 'Anyway, he has no reason to put a spoke in my wheel this time.'

'Except that he dislikes you,' she threw at him.

'He'd have disliked anyone you married,' he said. 'I expect to find him far more amenable the second time around.'

She said with difficulty, 'Of course—there's the contract. You—you have the upper hand now. I was forgetting.'

His smile wasn't pleasant. 'Unlike kindly Uncle Martin. He has a great deal to remember these days.'

'He looks ill,' she said bitterly. 'He isn't a young man, Jason. Couldn't you find yourself a worthier adversary?'

His smile deepened. 'Oh, but I have, sweetness,' he told her gently. He picked up her hand, kissed her soft palm, then released her, turning and walking back to the french windows and out into the sunlit garden.

Laura drew a deep shuddering breath, then sank down on the sofa burying her face in her hands. She felt shattered, her senses and emotions in shreds. She couldn't think straight, but out of the incoherencies whirling in her head came the certainty that it would be better if Jason did not come back and find her cowering here still, like a wounded animal.

She forced herself to the door, and out into the hall, intent on reaching her room. She was halfway up the stairs when she remembered her precious advertisements, and with a little groan, ran down again.

In the kitchen, Mrs Fraser was looking miffed.

'I wish Miss Celia would advise me of her plans rather earlier,' she said. 'I'd no idea there's to be guests tonight, and I only hope there are enough cutlets to go round.'

'Well, I shan't be here for dinner,' Laura said. 'So that should make everything right again. Mrs Fraser—when you tidied the drawing room, did you find some newspapers and magazines, because they belong to me and I haven't finished with them yet.'

'I did.' Mrs Fraser nodded acidly. 'All over the sofa, they were. The room looked as if an earthquake had hit it. You'll find them by the door in the laundry room. I wasn't going to make a special trip to the dustbin with them,' she added disapprovingly.

'Of course not. Thank you,' Laura managed civilly, resisting an unholy impulse to spit in the housekeeper's eye. She wondered if Mrs Fraser had seen all the little pencilled circles and drawn her own conclusions, but there was nothing in her demeanour to suggest this.

Laura retrieved the pile and carried it up to her room, stowing it in the recess under the window seat.

The familiar niggling battle with Mrs Fraser had restored her equanimity to some extent, and it still seemed that her only option was escape—and as soon as possible besides.

She would put as much distance between herself, this house, this family, this town—this man—as was humanly feasible.

And she would try to blot out from her consciousness the certain knowledge that however far she might travel, Jason would go with her, in her heart and in her mind.

CHAPTER NINE

IT had been a long hot journey, and a fruitless one, and Laura was tired as well as despondent as she drove through the lanes. She'd been for an interview to a private residential home for the elderly in a neighbouring county. They'd advertised for a cook/general help and Laura had guessed as soon as she arrived that the duties would probably include lending a hand with the heavy nursing. She'd been chilled to the bone by the comfortless lounge, and the sad, hopeless faces she saw there, and worried by the evasive answers which the proprietress had returned to her careful questions about diet and nutrition.

She'd already come to the reluctant conclusion that she and Mrs Fitzsimmons were never likely to get along when the only qualified nurse in the establishment had muttered out of the corner of her mouth, 'It's a dogsbody she wants, dear. There's precious little cooking goes on at this place, poor old beggars.'

It was almost a relief to have been told that Mrs Fitzsimmons felt an older person would be more suitable, even though it was a response which set her teeth on edge.

Perhaps I should be less fussy, she told herself miserably. Perhaps I should have ignored the fact that all I could see in the kitchens were fish fingers and huge cartons of instant mashed potato, and sold myself to that awful woman.

And perhaps pigs might fly, the other half of her mind returned succinctly.

But a wasted journey was always dispiriting, especially in view of the fact that it was still too early to return home. She'd managed to convey the impression to Celia that she was off to visit an old school friend, so she wouldn't be expected back for several hours yet.

She glanced at her watch. If she took the next left fork, she'd find her way to one of the local inns situated on the river. She could sit in the garden and watch the water flow under the little stone bridge while she had a quiet drink and contemplated what her next move should be. And later, she could eat there, too, which solved another problem.

It's ridiculous, she told herself, all this lurking round the countryside, but it was also inevitable. If Celia had the slightest inkling what she was up to, Laura knew she would tell Jason immediately, and she did not want him to know anything.

She tried to argue with herself over and over again that even if he did know, he would probably be totally unconcerned—might even think 'good riddance', but a more compelling instinct told her that he wouldn't let her escape him so easily. That he would try somehow to put a spoke in her wheel, for his own incomprehensible reasons.

And that was what she had to guard against at all costs. That and the danger that she might be tempted to stay, waiting on the fringe of his existence, hoping against hope . . .

She tore her mind back to the here and now, and realised, swearing mildly under her breath, that she had missed her turning. It wasn't a disaster, there was another crossroads a few miles further on, just past . . .

Just past Mill Cottage.

The car was already slowing to the pressure of her foot on the brake when she shook herself mentally. Now that really was ridiculous. She coudn't spend the rest of her time in the locality, weaving her way through the lanes in order to avoid one house.

Nor would Jason be there anyway, she realised. It

was far too early in the evening. He was working late more and more, to Celia's open annoyance, and none of her usual ploys from coaxing to sulks had produced the slightest alteration in any of his plans.

If he intended to marry her, Laura supposed that it was only right Celia should know from the start what she would have to contend with. But if she imagined the company would be her only rival for his attentions, then she would be bitterly wrong, Laura thought with a little sigh.

Celia had been disgruntled too that Jason hadn't allowed her a free, or, in fact, any sort of hand with the alterations and re-decoration which had been going on at Mill Cottage. He'd hired a top London firm, but had made it clear that they were working on his instructions and his alone. If they hadn't hurt so much, Laura would have found Celia's efforts to mask her baffled resentment almost amusing.

As the remnants of the mill ruins came in sight, she found herself tensing, her fingers gripping the wheel nervously. But she was worrying for nothing. The place was empty, of course. In fact, for all she knew Jason wasn't even living there yet. She always tried to switch off whenever Celia raised the subject of Jason's activities in front of her.

But there was someone at the cottage she realised with dismay as the car rounded the last slight curve in the lane. There was an estate car parked on the grass verge in front of the low front wall, and a woman's slim figure was moving about, taking things out of the boot.

At the sound of Laura's engine, she turned, shading her eyes against the sun, and Laura recognised with a sinking heart that it was Clare Marshall and that she was waving and clearly expecting her to stop.

Reluctantly she did so, but kept her engine running.

'What a pleasant surprise.' The other woman smiled at her as if it was true. 'Were you coming to visit us?'

'Er—no.' Laura knew she was flushing, and hated herself for it. 'On the contrary, I was on my way to the Wild Goose and missed the turning . . .'

It might be the truth but it sounded feeble in the extreme. Clare Marshall gave her a coaxing look. 'It's still very early. Wouldn't you like a coffee—or better still a lager? I put some in the 'fridge when I first arrived.'

Laura swallowed. 'I really couldn't put you to all that trouble . . .' she began, but Clare interrupted firmly. 'It's no trouble at all. I'd love some company. I've left the children with some friends for the weekend so that I could come down and get my part of the house straight. The decorators left yesterday and I'm dying to show it all to someone.' She grimaced. 'Lugging boxes around loses its savour after a very short time. I'm dying for an excuse to take a break. Please?'

Almost before she was aware what she was doing, Laura had reached for the door handle, and was following Clare up the path towards the front door. But they didn't use it. Instead Clare led the way round the side of the house.

'I have my own entrance,' she threw over her shoulder. 'The ladies who owned the place previously had the former stable converted into staff accommodation—I gather they had various married couples looking after the house and grounds for them—and it needed very little doing to it to make it suitable for the children and myself.'

She opened a green door on to a small vestibule smelling of fresh paint. 'See—completely self-contained.'

Laura looked around her with bewilderment. 'You're not living in the house itself?' She spoke the thought before she could stop herself, and paused, embarrassed. 'I mean . . .'

'Hardly.' Clare looked neither self-conscious nor

affronted. 'Jason is reasonably indulgent towards the children, but that doesn't mean he's prepared to have them underfoot all day long.'

Laura said feebly, 'I suppose not.'

She followed Clare into the kitchen. It wasn't large, but the new units gleamed and a stainless steel sink winked beneath the window.

'It's all rather pristine at the moment, but the kids will soon give it that lived in look.' Clare opened the 'fridge door. 'Which is it to be—coffee or lager?'

'Lager, please,' Laura said with a mental shrug. There was no reason on earth why Clare Marshall should offer her hospitality, or why she should accept it, yet here they both were, incredible though it seemed. She took the tall cool glass which Clare proffered with a brief word of thanks.

There was a pause, then she said, 'You'll find it very quiet here—after London.'

'Perhaps.' Clare gave a slight shrug. 'I'm looking forward to being settled, however. And I expect to be busy. Oh—not looking after the cottage. My duties as housekeeper are going to be purely nominal from what I can gather. Jason's already arranged for a daily woman to come in from the village. But I'm starting work again, as soon as the studios are complete.'

'Work?' Laura looked at her enquiringly.

'Why, yes. I used to work as an architect with Tristans'. Didn't you know?'

'I think I heard it mentioned.' Laura drank some more of her beer hastily.

'Well, I'm on the design strength again,' Clare said cheerfully. 'Only, I shall work from here instead of going into the new offices because of the children.'

'You mentioned studios . . .' Laura ventured after another pause.

'They're the next project,' Clare said briskly. 'They're

going to be at the other side of the house where those old outbuildings and that tumbledown greenhouse are now—one for Jason and one for myself.' She grinned. 'And has there been some skin and hair flying over the layout. Just like the old days when we both started at Tristans'. We never agreed even then.'

Laura forced a smile in return. 'It must have been stimulating,' she managed to say lightly.

'It had its moments.' The reminiscent expression in Clare's eyes made Laura's heart clench in the painful ugliness of jealousy.

She pushed back her chair and stood up, 'Well, thanks for the beer. I must be going . . .'

'Oh, not yet.' Clare rose too, firmly back in the present. 'I want to show you round. Have you ever been here before? Did you know the Misses Dainton?'

'Only by sight. They didn't go out a great deal.' Laura cast a surreptitious glance at her watch. A swift tour of Clare's flat and an even swifter departure, she thought. She could always say she was meeting someone at the Wild Goose.

She still found it hard to believe that she was actually here in the cottage chatting to Clare as if they were recent acquaintances who might become friends, as if no deep seas of bitterness existed to keep them on opposing shores.

As she followed Clare upstairs, she found herself thinking, 'Why is she doing this when she has as little reason to like me as I have to like her, both of us interlopers in the other's life?'

'None of the rooms up here are large,' Clare was saying. 'So I decided to take the smallest, which is really a boxroom, and let Jason and Elizabeth have whatever space was available.'

A single bed in the boxroom, Laura noticed, with a dainty sprigged bedcover to match the curtains and wallpaper. Could this be Clare's way of hinting to her that she didn't intend to spend many of her nights in this cramped space?

Past the constriction in her throat, she said, 'Your children have nice names.'

Clare shrugged lightly. 'Rather conventional, really. Jason was named for his father, of course. And my mother's name was Elizabeth. They'll be taking up residence next week when I've had time to unpack some of their toys and other things to make it home for them. Then they can spend the rest of the summer making friends with their new surroundings before Jason starts at the village school in September.'

Laura's lips felt wooden. 'I hear it's a very good school.' There was a framed photograph of the children standing on a chest of drawers, a studio portrait, the two dark heads posed close together, the cast of their features unmistakable. She felt a little moan welling up inside her, and had to clench her fists, digging her nails into the palms of her hands to regain her self control.

'I've heard so too,' Clare said cheerfully. 'In fact I'm hoping that I can ignore the fact there's a trust fund set up for their education, and use the local facilities. I hate the idea of waving them off to boarding schools, however good.' She glanced at Laura. 'Are you all right? You're very pale.'

Laura said, 'It's very warm up here. No air.'

Clare said with compunction, 'I haven't had time yet to open the windows, and you're right—it is stifling. Here.' She took Laura's arm and guided her down the steep flight to the ground floor. 'I know what you need.' She produced a key from her pocket and unlocked a door facing them. 'Some brandy.'

She steered Laura firmly over the threshold and across a stone-flagged hallway, and pushed open another door. 'In you go.'

It was a large room, at least double the size of any she had just visited. Oriental rugs gleamed like jewels on the stone floor, and attractively mullioned windows were provided with cushioned seats from which to look out at the gardens. A leather chesterfield stood facing an imposing stone fireplace, and one wall was lined with glass fronted bookcases in dark oak.

Laura said hoarsely, 'Whose side of the house is this?'

'Jason's.' Clare was unlocking an antique corner cupboard, and extracting a bottle. 'Like it?'

Laura moistened her lips with the tip of her tongue. 'It's beautiful. Look—I must be going—really. I don't need any brandy. I'm feeling better already.'

Clare's gaze was critical. 'You look like a ghost. Sit down while I fetch a glass and—oh damn,' she broke off in vexation. 'That's my telephone. I'll be back in two seconds.'

She put the bottle down on a low table in front of the chesterfield and vanished.

Laura thought, 'This is my chance to vanish too.'

She felt wretched and ill at ease, yet underneath there was an odd excitement too.

Bluebeard's wife, she thought, and smiled a little bitterly, as she turned towards the door.

She stopped short, the breath catching in her throat.

He was there—inevitably. Standing in the doorway watching her. Trapping her.

He said, 'I thought I recognised the other car.' He strolled forwards, his ironic gaze studying the brandy. 'Is this a private party or can anyone join in?'

She said almost inaudibly, 'I felt ill—Clare offered . . .'

'Then I can do no less. Where is Clare by the way?'

'The telephone . . .'

'I see.' There was the sound of approaching footsteps, and he glanced over his shoulder. He said, 'I got back early. I'll look after Laura and see her on her way.'

'Fine.' Clare sounded almost casual. 'When you want

to eat there's cold chicken and salad in the 'fridge. 'Bye.'

In the ensuing stillness, Laura heard the communicating door close, and the sound of the key being turned.

She said hoarsely, 'I have to go. You—you must wonder what I'm doing here.'

'Not particularly.' He shook his head. 'I imagine you were driving past, and your curiosity got the better of you. I hope my inopportune appearance hasn't spoiled the guided tour.'

She said with a creditable assumption of coolness, 'I've seen all that I want to see. And now I'd like to be on my way.'

'Without your medicinal brandy.' He shook his head. 'That would never do. Or would you prefer to join me in a whisky and soda?'

'I don't want a drink at all.' He was still blocking the doorway. She said, 'Jason—please I want to leave now.'

'And I want you to stay.' He sounded faintly amused. 'Impasse. And not for the first time.'

'But hopefully for the last.' She walked to the chesterfield and sat down, smoothing her skirt over her knees with a gesture that she realised too late was purely nervous. She stared straight ahead of her at the massive fireplace and its empty grate. 'Do we have to keep playing these games? Doesn't it bother you that she—that Clare will be—wondering what we're saying to each other? That this could be hurting her?'

'Frankly, no. I don't regard it as any of her concern,' he said bitingly.

Her head turned slowly, and she stared at him. 'Just what kind of a man are you?' Her voice trembled. 'Do you think that—providing a roof over their heads—expensive school fees—is all that it takes? That it entitles you to lock them all into a separate part of the house—to pretend that they don't have any feelings. Is that what would have happened to me if I'd stayed married to you? Would I have been locked away in the end in some little separate compartment labelled "wife"?'

He shook his head. 'No need, my darling. You'd already locked yourself away in a place where no-one could reach you. Oh, once or twice, I thought I'd finally broken through the shell and reached the loving, trusting girl I believed might be there inside it, but it was all myth, wasn't it, Laura? You wanted to be alone. You never really wanted me or our marriage or you'd have fought for me when that lying old hypocrite started dropping his poison in your ear. But you listened. You swallowed every bloody word, because it was your excuse to be out, to retreat back into your ivory tower—to be "Laura alone" again.'

She pressed her hands over her ears, terrified at the fierce wave of words breaking over her. 'Don't—it isn't true.'

His voice was cruel. 'And what would you know about the truth? I'll show you the truth.'

He strode across the room and grasped her arm, his fingers biting into the flesh as he hauled her to her feet.

Her voice broke on a sob. 'Jason—for God's sake, let me go.'

He said savagely, 'In my own good time. Not feeling faint again, are you, darling? Perhaps I'd better take the brandy with us, in case I need to revive you.'

His arm clamped round her waist, hurting her, as he lifted her off her feet as if she'd been a small child and carried her to the door.

One of her sandals dropped to the floor and was left. Her clenched fists pummelled at his shoulder. She tried to scratch his face.

'Put me down, damn you, you bastard.'

He stopped, changing his hold on her without releasing her. Laura found herself, to her horror, tucked under his arm, her head dangling helplessly towards the floor as he carried her up the stairs. Against his strength she was like a puppet, a rag doll, and the position she was in made her head swim.

'Brute,' she sobbed breathlessly.

He didn't reply. She wondered if he'd gone mad.

At the top of the stairs, he put her down. Unbalanced by the fact that she only wore one sandal, she staggered, but he seemed not to notice. Grasping her wrist, he pulled her, limping, along the landing to a door at the end. He threw it open. And almost threw her inside.

He was breathing hard, a white line round his mouth, his eyes brilliant with a flame that dazzled her.

He said, 'There it is, Laura. There's the truth. I keep it above my bed as a constant reminder of how wrong I can be.'

It was the portrait he had painted of her. She looked up dazedly at the girl in the patchwork skirt which she had been. She remembered the shyness, the agony of loneliness which she believed had gone forever in his arms and a deep choking sob welled up from inside her.

He heard the sound she made and turned towards her impatiently, his face harsh. 'Now who's playing games?' There was silence as he registered her trembling lips and tear-misted eyes. His voice sank to a groan. 'Laura—dear God—Laura . . .'

He began to kiss her, his mouth brushing gently on her own as if in recompense for his earlier harshness, and for a while it was enough for her to stand in the circle of his arms, and allow these featherlight caresses on her mouth, her eyes, her cheeks and forehead. To feel the pain and the bitterness drain out of her as if his touch had the power to heal her. As perhaps it did, she thought from the strange dream which enfolded her. Only now it was time for the dreaming to stop.

She moved slowly, moulding her body against his, watching the concern in his eyes change to hunger as she offered him her parted lips.

This time he wasn't gentle, but desire was running through her like a flame and she responded to his passionate possession of her mouth with equal fierceness, her hands going up to clasp the back of his head, and hold him to her.

By the time he took his mouth from hers, she was breathless, her senses going crazy, her pulses clamouring.

He released her and stepped one step backwards, his eyes watching her with a challenge as old as time. He shrugged off the expensive jacket and let it fall to the floor, tugged his tie loose, and dry-mouthed she remembered the first time she had watched him undress, excitement warring with a measure of fearfulness. But she wasn't that apprehensive girl any longer. She was a woman now, with needs and urgencies too long unsatisfied.

She moved to him. He was unbuttoning his shirt, but he paused, brows lifted, as she pushed his hands away and took over the task herself. His skin was warm, and she pressed her mouth against him, letting the familiarity of the taste, the scent of him wash into her eager consciousness. She could feel the race of his heartbeat under her lips, the stir of his aroused body against hers. He took her face in his hands and kissed her hotly and deeply. Her head fell back, letting his lips trace the slender line of her throat down to the unfastened collar of her dress. His hands moved releasing the remaining buttons, opening her dress to the waist. Her body shivered with delight as his fingers delicately explored her breasts, freeing them from the fragile lace cups of her bra for the pleasure of kisses.

He undid the remaining buttons, then pushed the dress gently from her shoulders. It fell to the floor to be joined a second later by her lacy half slip.

He lifted her and put her on the bed, following her

down on to the yielding surface and kissing her with slow, sensuous pleasure while his caressing hands completed her undressing. When she felt him move away, she knew a moment of panic, remembering how he had rejected her that night at Alan's cottage, but almost before the thought had formulated he was beside her again, naked himself now. Her hands touched his long, muscular back, embracing him fiercely, adoring the warmth and strength of him in her arms.

Nothing else mattered but the heated tide of sensation rising within her, the overwhelming need for fulfilment which he aroused in her.

His mouth tantalised her, moving with unhurried eroticism down her body, following the path of pleasure his exploring fingers had already traced. She caressed him too, touching him with lingering intimacy in the ways that he had taught her.

She was on fire for him, and when at last his body covered hers, she welcomed the first fierce thrust of his possession with wild savage sweetness, moving with him, responding to him so that the taking was mutual and overwhelming. Her cry of ecstatic release was echoed by his own, and still twined together, they fell asleep.

Some time later, she was aware she was being lifted, that there was now a pillow under her head, and the softness of a quilt covering her. She murmured something happily and slept again.

When she woke properly, the room was dark.

For a moment Laura lay there savouring the feeling of voluptuous well-being pervading her entire body, and wondering why she felt so wonderful—then she remembered, and sat up with a stifled gasp, her hand flying to her mouth.

She was alone now, although the rumpled pillow beside her told its own story. As she crouched there tensely in the silent darkness she heard faint sounds from the downstairs—someone moving about, the chink of crockery.

She'd fallen into the very trap, she had sworn to avoid, and hot shame engulfed her at the realisation. Like a frightened child she drew her knees up to her chin, wrapping her arms tightly round them while she tried to think what to do.

There was no excuse for what she had done. None at all. She had known from the first moment that Jason had come back into her life that he still had the most devastating effect on her. Self-respect at least had demanded that she should keep him at a distance, or at least pretend that all desire was dead, but her body had betrayed her every time and he was far too experienced not to have known this, and capitalised on it, she thought bitterly. She had fallen into his arms like a starving animal scenting food.

She cast a despairing glance at the digital clock on one of the low tables which flanked the big bed. It was past midnight, and her car was parked outside for anyone to see. For Clare Marshall to see and draw her own conclusions.

Laura groaned, throwing back the covers and swinging her legs to the floor. She clicked on one of the tall cream-shaded lamps and began to search hurriedly for her clothing, disentangling it from Jason's with hands that shook.

She wasted several minutes hunting around for her other sandal, remembering at last that she had lost it downstairs. Holding the remaining sandal, she tiptoed down to the hall and into the drawing room, hastily retrieving her missing footwear from beside the sofa.

She was on her way down the hall to the front door, when a door opened behind her and light flooded out.

Jason said, 'Laura? Where the hell are you going?'

She turned slowly and reluctantly. For a moment he was just a dark silhouette framed in the bright kitchen doorway, then he moved towards her and she saw that he was carrying a tray. She saw dishes with chicken and salad, a tall green bottle of wine, glasses, a rose in a silver vase. He put the tray down on a side table, and stood looking at her. He was wearing a towelling bathrobe, his bare feet thrust into heelless leather mules.

He said quietly, 'What is this? Where are you going?'

'Away from here. Home,' she said rather wildly, and his eyes narrowed.

'Come and have something to eat,' he invited. 'And we'll talk about it.'

'There's nothing to talk about,' she denied.

His brows snapped together. 'You can't be serious.'

'Never more so.' She drew a deep steadying breath. 'I—I can't undo the last few hours, Jason, but you must understand that I would if it were possible. I'll never forgive myself for what has happened.'

He was silent for a moment. 'And by the same token, I presume you don't intend to forgive me either,' he suggested drily.

'If you like. I don't want to discuss it.'

'Then I'm afraid you're going to have to force yourself,' his tone was implacable. 'I have you now, Laura, and you're not running out on me again. We're going to settle this whole miserable business once and for all no matter who gets hurt in the process.'

'No.' Laura shook her head desperately. 'I can't. I won't—and you're not going to make me.' She flung her head back. 'I'm leaving this place, Jason. I'm going away—getting a job.'

'You—are—what?' His voice deepened menacingly. 'What kind of a job?'

She shrugged. 'Cooking—housework—the things I know about.'

'And you think I'll allow this—allow my wife to become a drudge for some stranger . . .?'

She shook her head. 'There isn't a thing you can do about it. And I'm not your wife.'

'Not long ago,' he said slowly, 'you were all the wife any man on earth could ever want. You can't do this to us, Laura. Stay with me.'

'No.' The word almost choked out of her. 'Because I can't do this to—her.'

'Her?' He frowned again. 'If you mean Celia . . .'

'I don't. I mean Clare,' she threw at him. 'How do you think she feels—seeing my car still outside— knowing that we're here together. Or don't you care?'

'I don't give a damn,' he said. 'And I don't suppose she does either. Why not ask her?'

'Well, I care.' Her throat was tight with misery. 'I care like hell. I hate myself for what happened tonight. And I hate you too. I hope I never have to see you again.'

Her voice broke on a sob and she ran to the front door, tugging at the securing lock, praying inwardly that he wouldn't try to stop her.

Because she knew if he spoke her name just once more with that heart-stopping tenderness, or touched her, then her new-found resolve would crumble away to nothingness, and she would stay with him forever, be what he wanted, do what he wanted.

But only silence followed her. Somehow she made her way to the car, found the bag she'd left lying on the seat all those hours before, found her keys, started the engine.

Drove away into the bleakness and loneliness of the night.

CHAPTER TEN

When Laura opened her eyes, it took a few moments to remember where she was and how she'd got there.

Bethany and Mike had still been clearing up when she arrived at the restaurant, tense and drawn. Miraculously they'd asked no questions, refused to listen to her stumbling explanations, simply made her have a warm drink while Bethany made up the spare room bed.

'We'll talk in the morning,' Bethany had promised, firmly clicking off the light and closing the door behind her.

Now, Laura wasn't so sure that was a good idea. What could she say after all? How could she rationally explain her conduct?

She got up and dressed, and went rather reluctantly to find her hosts. In the living room, she discovered Mike sitting at the table in the window, going over some accounts.

He smiled at her. 'Beth's had to pop out, love. Coffee?'

'I'd love some.' Laura slid into the seat opposite, watching as he filled another cup from the steaming pot beside him. She said, 'Mike, I'm sorry about last night. It was unforgivable, landing on you like that and . . .'

Mike held up a hand. 'Let's hold it right there, my pet. We're your friends, and we're here to help, but not pry. If you needed a sanctuary last night, then that's as much as we need to know, and that goes for Bethany as well.'

Laura's eyes filled with tears. 'Oh God, I don't deserve you.'

'There are various schools of thought on that too,' Mike said solemnly, handing her a clean handkerchief. 'Talking of old friends,' he added, after a pause during which Laura took a firm grip on her self-control, 'one of yours was in here last night. Guy called Alan.'

'Oh,' Laura said guiltily. 'I—I have rather a conscience about him.'

'Then you don't need to have,' Mike assured her kindly. 'He was accompanied by a rather plump redhead who was hanging on his every word. Beth said she would obviously rather have been having him for dinner than any of our delicious food. Looked incredibly pleased with himself,' he added caustically.

'Then I hope it all works out for him,' Laura said slowly. 'He—he was a nice person basically.'

'But not for you,' Mike completed for her, and she smiled sadly.

'No, not for me.' She was silent for a moment, then said with an assumption of cheerfulness. 'Well, I can't sit here doing nothing. Let me write out the menus for next week.'

'If you want,' Mike said amiably. 'Although I've no objection to you doing nothing. You do it very decoratively.'

He fetched the draft and the cards and the black ink, and she sat, concentrating on producing a perfect italic script. She was halfway through when Bethany's footsteps came running up stairs.

'It's hell in town,' she announced as she burst into the room. 'Hot and crowded.' She sat down, kicking off her shoes. 'Feeling better?' Her eyes were fixed on Laura with a shade of anxiety in their clear depths. 'How did that interview go?'

Interview, Laura thought puzzled, then her brain cleared and she remembered Mrs Fitzsimmons and the sad old ladies. She grimaced. 'Another disaster. Not that I should have let that weigh with me,' she added.

'A job is a job, and I'm getting desperate. I'm going to take the next one that offers, no matter what the snags.'

There was a pause, then Bethany said, 'If you really mean that, then perhaps I could help.'

'You already have—above and beyond the call of duty.' Laura smiled at her. 'You know I can't work here on a permanent basis. I've explained why . . .'

'I didn't mean that,' Bethany said. There was an odd note in her voice. 'I wasn't sure whether to mention this or not—but it could be the answer for you.' She took a breath. 'One of our customers has an elderly relative—a grandmother who's looking for a cook housekeeper right at this moment. The last one has had to leave in a hurry—from what I can gather her father's had a heart attack and she's needed to look after him, which has left this old lady in rather a spot.'

'But how do you know all this?' Laura felt bewildered.

'The grand-daughter was telling me about it last night.' Bethany fiddled with her wedding ring. 'Asking me if I knew of anyone. Apparently the old lady has arthritis quite badly and has a nurse companion living with her, so there'd be two to cook for most of the time, although she enjoys good food and likes to give occasional dinner parties.' She hesitated. 'It seemed heaven-sent, Laurie, so I—I took the address, if you want it.'

She hunted through her bag and produced a slip of paper.

'Near Warwick,' Laura commented half to herself. 'Well, that should be far enough away. It sounds ideal.'

'Yes.' Bethany was unhappy and showed it. 'Oh, Laurie, I hope I've done the right thing by mentioning it. I'm so confused—but you look so—so sad that I can't bear it.'

Mike said to no-one in particular, 'I'll make some fresh coffee,' and faded tactfully out of the room.

'But this could be just what I need—a fresh start,' Laura urged persuasively, looking with concern at her friend's downbent head.

Bethany roused herself with an effort. 'Perhaps. I wish I could be sure. But anything's better than this limbo you've been occupying lately.'

Laura stared at her. 'Anything? Do you know something I don't? Is Grandma a tartar—the terror of the servants' quarters?'

Bethany smiled a little. 'I don't think so. Her present cook has been with her for fifteen years. It should be a good sign. I—I didn't ask too many questions because I didn't know how you'd react—if you'd be interested.'

'I'm more than interested.' Laura stowed the address purposefully in her bag, 'I'll write as soon as I get home. Thank you, Beth.'

Bethany gave her a quick fierce hug. 'I don't want thanks. I just want you to be happy. I only hope this is the way . . .'

Driving back to the house, Laura thought that Bethany's qualms were quite understandable. She was too lively herself to appreciate that anyone could be happy burying themselves in the wilds of Warwickshire with an arthritic and possibly demanding old lady. She would think it a retrograde step, even as a temporary measure.

For herself, Laura hoped that this unknown Mrs Chesterfield would be demanding.

I hope she keeps me running, she thought. I hope I don't have a moment to think—to brood.

She parked the car, and ran into the house, taking the stairs two at a time, only to come face to face with Celia at the top.

'So you're back,' her cousin said slowly, looking her over.

'As you see,' Laura returned.

'I see more than you think.' Celia moved, blocking

Laura's path deliberately. 'Daddy may have been taken in by your story of an old school friend, but I'm not. Where were you last night?'

Laura shrugged. 'I went for an interview for a job,' she said. 'It was late when I got back so I stopped over with Bethany and Mike. You can check if you want,' she added.

'That won't be necessary,' Celia said sharply, but there was an underlying note of relief there too. 'What do you mean—a job? You already have one here.'

'Not for much longer,' Laura said pleasantly. 'From now on this house is all yours—and Mrs Fraser's of course. I wish you joy of each other.'

'Does my father know?' Celia demanded.

Laura nodded. 'Yes.'

'Well.' Celia gave a short laugh. 'You seem to have it all cut and dried. Perhaps you're wise too. It can't be very nice for you to have to watch while the man you were once married to falls in love with someone else.'

Laura lifted her brows satirically. 'Is that what's happening?'

Celia gave her a venomous look. 'Yes, it is. Jason and I are going to be married, and I think we'd both prefer it if you were not around. You do rather tend to be the skeleton at the feast, sweetie, even if you don't care about him any more. I think it would be less embarrassing for everyone if you were to take yourself off.'

'I'm sure you're right, and that's exactly what I intend.' Celia's malice made her cringe, but Laura maintained a smiling front. 'So—if you'll excuse me . . .'

'Of course.' Celia gave ground gracefully, her expression reflecting her satisfaction. She moved towards the stairs then halted. 'There—I almost forgot. Daddy rang not long ago asking for you. He said, when you came in you were to join him at the factory. Apparently today's the make or break meeting with

Tristans. No doubt he wants you to soften their hearts with a delicious lunch. Have fun.'

She went on downstairs, and presently Laura heard her car driving away. She fought a brief inner battle, then went down to the hall and telephoned the works, asking for Fergie.

'I hear I'm wanted,' she said, when she'd been put through. 'What is it? Another last minute lunch?'

'Oh, Laura.' Fergie sounded harassed. 'No—it's nothing to do with food, as far as I know. Mr Caswell wants to see you as soon as possible, he says. Can you come at once?'

Laura sighed. 'I suppose so,' she said resignedly. 'What's it about?'

'I wish I knew,' Fergie moaned. 'This meeting with the Tristan board started at nine and adjourned about half an hour ago. They're all having coffee in separate offices at the moment. They all look very grim and I can only think it's going badly. Your uncle looks really ill. And we've had the newspapers on asking if we'll have to close down if we lose this contract.'

'Good God.' Laura was appalled. She made up her mind. 'I'll be straight over.'

She put down the receiver and thought for a moment. If she didn't write her letter, she would miss the post. On the other hand, the address slip which Bethany had given her did have a telephone number.

Nothing ventured, she thought, and dialled.

A woman's voice answered, firm and pleasant, and Laura asked for Mrs Chesterfield.

'She's resting at the moment,' came the reply. 'I'm Miss Bishop, her companion. Is there anything I can do?'

Rather haltingly, Laura explained. 'I would have written,' she concluded. 'But I got the impression from—from my informant that the matter was urgent.'

'It certainly is,' Miss Bishop sounded brisk. 'My cooking skills are confined to a hundred things to do with an egg, and we miss Marjorie dearly. Would it be possible for you to come for an interview tomorrow. Naturally, your expenses would be paid. Shall we say two o'clock?'

'That would be fine,' Laura said. 'I'll bring my references.'

'You do that,' said Miss Bishop. 'And if they're satisfactory, be prepared to stay on and cook dinner for us. We're in dire need of a square meal,' she added plaintively.

In spite of everything, Laura found she was smiling as she put the 'phone down. Miss Bishop didn't sound the sort of woman who would work for an ogress, she told herself optimistically. She would pack her case and take it with her, in case they wanted her to start at once. She could always send for the rest of her things later.

As she drove into the factory car park, she remembered that this was how it all began. Suddenly, unbelievably Jason had been back in her life, upsetting everything, destroying the fragile security she thought she had found.

Arriving at the floor where the executive offices were sited, she found Fergie waiting restlessly for her.

'Thank heavens you're here,' she exclaimed as Laura emerged from the lift. 'If he's asked for you once, he's asked a dozen times. The meeting's due to start again in a few minutes, and he's sitting in his office refusing to take any calls. I've never known anything like it.'

Laura heard her in dismay. Uncle Martin had always coped with each and every crisis as it arose. But he was no longer a young man, and clearly the stress and strain of the past weeks had taken its toll of him as well.

He wasn't at his desk as she went into his office. He was occupying one of the big leather easy chairs reserved for visitors, his body slumped.

For a moment he looked at her as she spoke his

name, as if he didn't know who she was. Then he said in a thin voice. 'Sit down my dear child.'

She knelt instead beside him, taking his hand in hers, feeling with alarm that he was shaking.

She said gently, 'You're not well, darling. Shall I tell these people to come back another day?'

'No,' he said with something like his old force. 'Laura—you told me you intended to take a job away from here. Have you succeeded in finding anything suitable?'

She could hardly believe it. She said levelly, 'I think so, Uncle, but this is hardly the appropriate time to talk about it. We'll discuss it tonight, if you wish . . .'

'It has to be now,' he said heavily. 'Laura, I don't wish to see you dependent on strangers for your living. It was your father's wish—indeed it's my wish to see you provided for from this company.'

'But I already am.' Laura began to feel she was living in a dream. 'I've had an income ever since I was eighteen.'

'But only a pittance by today's standards.' He looked down at the floor, not meeting her gaze. 'It has to be increased so that you have enough to live on comfortably if—if this job you take should turn out to be—unsuitable. And there's a lump sum too, for you to invest.'

Laura tugged at his sleeve. 'Uncle Martin—I don't want this money. I don't need it. I'm capable of earning my own living, and I have no intention of becoming a Caswells' pensioner. Besides, the way things are the company can't afford to be paying me that kind of money for nothing.'

'But when the contract is signed, everything will be different,' he said. 'You must take it, Laura. For your father's sake, if nothing else. It's what he intended, after all.'

She said gently, 'Daddy wouldn't have wanted me to sponge from Caswells when there was no need.'

'Then do it for me.' The wretched expression in his eyes shocked her. 'Laura, my dear, you don't realise how—very—important this is for me. For us all.'

Laura sat back on her heels. She said, 'Why is it so important? What haven't you told me? What's happened?'

He said heavily, 'Your ex-husband insists that adequate financial provision is made for you. That's the condition on which the Tristan contract rests. He spoke to me privately first thing this morning, told me unless I agreed, the negotiations would stop. Warned me that until it was officially arranged, cleared with you, that he wouldn't proceed.'

Laura got to her feet. She was shaking now. She said, 'He has no right. No right at all. Uncle Martin you aren't going to submit to this—blackmail. I won't allow it. He can't interfere like this. I don't want the money.' Her voice rose.

Her uncle looked up at her, his face drawn. 'But it's yours, my dear.'

'On Jason's say so?' She laughed scornfully. 'No way.'

He shook his head. He looked old and weary. 'By the terms of your father's will. He made provision for you from his half of the business, but left it in trust, so that you would receive extra income when you married, and the remainder as a lump sum when you gave birth to your first child.'

It was a warm day. The office was filled with sunshine, but suddenly Laura felt cold.

She said slowly, 'This is the first I've heard of it.'

Martin Caswell went on half to himself, 'I was the trustee with old Harrington, but he died two years later. You were only a child, too young to understand about such things, so I never explained it to you in full. I promised myself that I would when you were older. There seemed no hurry, and in the meantime the money was there to be used—for Caswells. Only—things started to go wrong. There was a recession. Money was tight. We could keep our heads above water, but only just or so I told myself. That was why—when you got married so suddenly—I didn't say anything. I—I persuaded myself that the company couldn't afford to pay you any more. I thought your husband was just a fly-by-night artist with no head for business. It never occurred to me that he would look up your father's will.'

She looked down at him, her heart thudding painfully. She said, 'You told me once that Jason had been to you—asking for money. You made it sound as if he'd been sponging from you. Was it . . .'

'Yes,' he said. 'He'd discovered the truth and came to confront me with it. I—I begged him not to tell you, and he agreed. He said it would only—hurt you to find I'd been cheating you, and he didn't want that. But I didn't believe him. I thought he would tell you, and I couldn't bear it. You'd been like my own child for so long. I didn't want anything to change that—to change your regard for me. I promised myself that whatever happened I would make it up to you in other ways. It was not long after that my enquiry agent found the Marshall woman and her child. They were exactly what I needed.'

It hurt to breathe. 'You broke up my marriage—for money?'

He winced. 'Laura you have to understand how it was. The company was in difficulties. To have been forced to pay out that kind of sum could have caused a crisis. I was at my wit's end.'

'You could have told me,' she said. 'I would have understood. Caswells was my father's company too. I wouldn't have agreed to anything which might damage its prospects. Didn't you know that?'

He shook his head slowly. 'I felt I—I couldn't take that risk.'

She shivered. 'And my baby? I suppose it was quite a relief when I lost it.'

He gave her an agonised look. 'Oh, my dear—no—never . . .'

'But it wouldn't have been very convenient for you—my being pregnant,' she said consideringly. 'And you certainly wouldn't have wanted it to happen again. If I—stopped being married—it would settle both problems. And providing me with a home would make me grateful—for small mercies. It did too. Kindly Uncle Martin,' she ended on a little shaken laugh.

'Laura—don't!' He looked and sounded appalled.

'Would you have ever told me the truth? I suppose not. It must have been an unpleasant shock when Jason returned—and in a position to dictate terms.' She shook her head. 'He said he'd make you pay—but I didn't understand.'

He said, 'I've paid every day since he returned. I couldn't even forbid him the house as I wanted—couldn't warn Celia. That was his price for remaining silent. And then—today—everything changed. He was angry—talked about you planning to become a household drudge—said that he'd do anything he could to prevent it. And then he delivered his ultimatum—either I paid over all the money I owed you—enabled you to become independent—or there would be no contract. I had to agree. We've gambled heavily on Fibrona—borrowed to put it into production. The cancellation would be a disaster—we couldn't pull through.'

Laura looked at him, her lip curling slightly. 'Oh, you'd find some way out, Uncle Martin. You're very resourceful, as I'm just beginning to realise.' She paused. 'Open an account in my name and pay the money into it, if that's what it takes. I shall never touch it. Tomorrow I shall be gone—and I'm never coming back.'

She turned and walked out of the room. Her head was high, but her eyes were unseeing with pain. As she reached the corridor, she stumbled slightly, and immediately Jason's arm was round her, steadying her.

He said abruptly, 'Come in here.'

A door opened. She looked round dazedly, and found they were in the deserted board room.

Jason closed the door and leaned against it, his eyes searching her face.

He said, 'So he told you. I didn't think he would.'

She folded her arms, wrapping them round her body. 'He had very little choice. I—I told him I wouldn't take the money. So—he had to explain why I should.' Her eyes met his. 'But it makes no difference. I still won't accept a penny.'

He said quietly, 'The money's yours, Laura. He cheated you out of it, and all under the guise of loving concern. He deserves to be dragged through the courts.'

She moved restively, 'No—I couldn't. But I can't take the money either. I want nothing from him. I just want to get away.'

'Then the money would help.'

'No.' Laura shook her head violently. 'It wouldn't. It would mean I was still connected—still dependent—and I don't want that. I'm going to be interviewed for a residential post tomorrow, and if it's offered, I shall take it.'

Jason's face darkened. 'I'm damned if you will. Haven't you been a drudge for long enough? I won't allow it.'

'It's none of your concern.' Her voice shook a little.

'You can stand there and say that,' he said slowly. 'For God's sake, Laura, you can't pretend last night meant nothing to you. I want you back. Why else do you think I've been haunting your uncle's bloody house for weeks, except to catch the occasional glimpse of you—to try and convince myself that in spite of everything you still cared about me.'

She said, 'But—Celia. You're going to marry her. She said—she thought . . .'

'To hell with Celia and what she says and thinks. I don't give a damn about her, or anyone but you. I never have. What do I have to do to convince you?'

'You have no right to say that.' The words were like stones in her throat. 'You have other responsibilities— other priorities. Do you expect me to simply forget that?' She flung back her head.

'No,' he said. 'But you don't understand my duty to Clare. You never have.'

'What is there to understand?' She moved her hands helplessly. 'I won't—share. If that's a fault in me, then I admit it. Even if I have to be alone for the rest of my life, I can't make room for another woman in our relationship. I can't live in that house—see her every day—see her children.' She bit her lip. 'Tell me something. If I asked you to send her away—would you?'

He said, 'I can't. Laura—I asked you once to trust me . . .'

She shook her head. 'I don't think I have any trust left—you and Uncle Martin—between you, you've used it all up.' She gave a small, unhappy smile. 'I'm not very lucky with the men in my life, it seems.'

He said expressionlessly. 'No. Goodbye, Laura. I wish you better fortune in the future.' He stood away from the door, opening it for her with a kind of remote courtesy that somehow hurt more than anger or bitterness would have done.

The corridor outside seemed full of people, all of them trying to conceal their curiosity and in most cases, failing miserably. She saw Bill Hurst, the company secretary, looking puzzled and concerned. He pushed his way to her side. 'Laura—what's going on? You look like a ghost and Martin's on the point of collapse.'

She gave him what she hoped was a reassuring smile. 'Everything's fine, Bill, honestly. My uncle's been under a lot of strain recently. Perhaps when all the business of the negotiations is over, you can persuade him to have a complete medical check up.'

He frowned, 'But surely, he would listen to you . . .'

'I shan't be here. I've got a job in Warwickshire.' She crossed her fingers in the folds of her skirt, hoping that it was true.

'I see.' Clearly he didn't, but was too polite to say so. 'Well—we will miss you.'

'Thank you.'

Behind her, she heard Jason say calmly, 'I'm sorry to have kept you waiting, gentlemen. Perhaps we could resume our meeting. After all we have a contract to sign.'

She saw the concern in Bill's face change to relief as his attention was dramatically diverted.

No-one gave her a second glance as she walked away down the corridor.

Behind her, she heard the hum of voices die away as the board room door closed, shutting her out.

She didn't look back but went on walking steadily down the corridor, away from everything she wanted most in the world, towards a future which had never seemed more empty.

CHAPTER ELEVEN

It was raining when Laura got to Warwick. The long hot spell was over, it seemed, and in some strange way the change in the weather signalled the dramatic alteration in her own circumstances.

She'd made good time, so she enjoyed a leisurely drive round Warwick, promising herself that she would come back and tour the castle when she had time.

And, of course, if she got this job, she reminded herself hastily. She'd burned her bridges fairly thoroughly, and if Mrs Chesterfield turned her down she wasn't sure what she would do instead.

Maybe she would stay in the area anyway, find herself a room, and live on her savings for a time while she looked for alternative employment. There seemed to be plenty of restaurants around—maybe one of them would need experienced help in the kitchen.

She tried to think optimistically, but it was difficult when her heart was breaking inside. It might be a cliché, but she could think of no better way of describing this tearing pain which made her every waking moment wretched, and even pursued her through her sleeping hours.

She was pale, and she had shadows under her eyes, and Mrs Chesterfield might well feel she didn't look nearly robust enough to take on a cook-housekeeper post.

Well, she would deal with that problem as and when it arose. She was here now, and here she would stay, and gradually the memories would fade, until eventually she might even be able to forget that the two men she had most loved had both callously betrayed her.

She found the house without difficulty. It was solid and dignified, made of red brick and set back from the road at the top of a tree-lined drive.

Laura parked decorously on the neatly raked gravelled forecourt and drew a deep breath as she mounted the two shallow steps which led to the front door.

Her ring at the bell was answered almost at once, as if they'd been waiting for her, watching for her arrival. Were they that desperate for a cook, she wondered wrily.

'I'm Wanda Bishop.' The voice on the telephone belonged to a tall woman with a calm face. Her handshake was firm and crisp, and shrewd eyes studied Laura. 'She's waiting for you. I'll take you straight in.' She paused. 'I'll give you about half an hour, then bring in tea. May I ask you to try not to agitate her too much? She is an invalid after all, and I can't truly say I approve of her seeing you.'

Laura groaned inwardly. Surely this pleasant looking woman wasn't another jealous, resentful Mrs Fraser, from whom she'd parted to their mutual satisfaction only a few hours before?

'I'll try,' she said levelly. 'Although it's difficult to see how I'm going to agitate someone with arthritis.'

'That's true.' Miss Bishop looked slightly amused. 'Only it isn't arthritis. She has a heart condition.'

She opened a door on the left of the hall and nodded Laura inside before she could ask anything else.

She felt totally bewildered. Bethany must have misunderstood, she thought. Perhaps it would have been more sensible if she'd had a talk with Mrs Chesterfield's grand-daughter first and checked up on the situation.

That was her first thought. Her second was that the woman seated in a high-backed wing chair by the window was hardly old enough to have an adult grand-daughter. Her dark hair had silver wings at the temples, and her face had a drawn look, but she was hardly more than middle-aged.

Laura realised she was staring and moved forward in embarrassment.

She said, 'Mrs Chesterfield? It's very good of you to see me without a preliminary letter.'

'On the contrary.' Mrs Chesterfield's voice was low and rather musical. She was staring too, taking in every inch of Laura from head to foot. Her smile was charming. 'I've been so much wanting to meet you at last—Laura.'

Laura stopped short. Her conversation with Miss Bishop had been brief, but she was certain her Christian name had never been mentioned.

She said slowly, 'You know my name?'

The older woman nodded. 'And I have you at a disadvantage, because you don't know mine.'

What on earth was she talking about? Laura's brows twisted in a frown. 'Have I come to the wrong house? I have an interview with a Mrs Chesterfield. I'm so sorry . . .'

'This is the house. Only my name is not Chesterfield.' Her face was rueful for a moment. 'We—I thought if I said I was Lady Wingard then you might not come.'

'Lady Wingard.' Laura stood very still.

'Yes, my dear. I'm your mother-in-law.'

Laura shook her head. Her brain was churning. She said, 'I have no mother-in-law. I'm no longer married.'

'I'm well aware of that. That's why it was arranged for you to come here today.'

'Arranged?' Laura almost choked. 'But Bethany said . . .'

'Is that your friend who owns the restaurant? I'm very grateful to her for her help, although my son tells me she wasn't easy to persuade. But he was able to convince her eventually that he has nothing but your well-being at heart.'

'How kind of him.' Laura felt blank with shock, but anger was kindling too. 'I think I'd better be going.'

'Oh, please don't run away.' Lady Wingard extended a thin hand, her face appealing. 'This isn't easy for me either, but I have to talk to you, Laura. I have to tell you things I swore I would never tell anyone. I've been so terribly at fault, but you must let me do what I can to make amends.' She paused, her eyes scanning Laura's rigid face. A faint sigh escaped her. 'You don't understand one word I'm saying, and why should you, after all? Please sit down. Please listen to me, if not for my sake, then for Jason's. He's been so loyal, so caring, when it would have served me right if he'd never had anything to do with me again.'

Laura sank down on to the edge of the chair Lady Wingard indicated.

She said, 'I don't think you and I have anything to say to each other, but I'm prepared to listen if that's all that will satisfy you.'

'It isn't.' Lady Wingard leaned forward, her dark eyes suddenly brilliant. 'What would satisfy me would be to see you and Jason together again—husband and wife.' She smiled. 'As my dear dragon has no doubt told you, my health is poor. I'd like to enjoy my grandchildren in the time I have left.'

Laura winced. 'I'm sorry—there's no possibility . . .' She hesitated, acutely embarrassed. 'Besides—you must know—you already have grandchildren.'

She saw pain in the dark eyes, and started up in alarm. 'You're not well. Let me call Miss Bishop . . .'

Lady Wingard's hand rose commandingly, halting her. She leaned back in her chair, eyes closed, biting nervously at her lip.

She said half to herself, 'I never imagined how hard this was going to be.' Her voice firmed. 'I married an ambitious man, Laura. Oh, I was in love with him, but it was the ambition that attracted me initially—the knowledge that he was going to be a success. Tristan Construction was nothing when he inherited it, but he built it, poured his heart into it, and I worked with him in those early years—at least until Jason was born. Then I took more of a back seat. As the company grew, our social contacts increased. I enjoyed that. I enjoyed entertaining and was good at it.' She paused, her face wry. 'Better, in fact, than I was at being a wife. I wasn't very well while I was carrying Jason—and afterwards—and I let it be an excuse. I'm sure I don't have to explain further.'

'No, indeed.' Laura was uncomfortable. 'Lady Wingard—you don't have to tell me any of this . . .'

'Ah, but I do—otherwise you might not understand what happened later. On the surface, we passed as a happily married couple—devoted, I think the word is—but under the surface there were already rifts. After a while I realised my husband was having an affair. I faced him with it, and he admitted it—admitted that it hadn't been the first. I made it clear that he could amuse himself as he wished as long as he was discreet. I also told him that I would never agree to a divorce. The laws at that time were rather different. He accepted this and we went on as before, presenting a successful front to the world. I was an excellent hostess—an asset to Tristans—and my husband treated me generously. He bought me the house I wanted—no——' she smiled faintly—'not this one. I had the right clothes—expensive jewellery—everything to contribute to the perfect image. But however much I might pretend, the truth was we were leading separate lives and sooner or later there was going to be a crisis.'

She paused and looked at Laura. 'The crisis came when a girl called Clare Marshall joined the firm. She'd been at university with Jason. They were friends, but not lovers. And—my husband fell in love with her.'

There was a tense silence, then Laura found her voice. 'Your husband.'

'Yes,' said Lady Wingard. 'It was instant, mutual and apparently overwhelming, although to give the girl her due she resisted at first—even handed her notice in at one point. But in the end, she became his mistress. She left Tristan Construction and went to live in a flat for which he paid the rent. Eventually, she found she was going to have a child, and my husband asked me to divorce him so that he could marry her. I refused. I told myself I was perfectly justified. I had a comfortable, even a luxurious life which I was not prepared to jeopardise. Also we'd learned that there was the possibility of a knighthood in the offing. The last thing we wanted was a scandal—especially a sordid divorce. I saw no reason why things could not go on as they were.'

She sighed. 'But, of course, they didn't. My husband wished to marry Miss Marshall. Our—civilised relationship deteriorated. Jason and his father had already quarrelled bitterly over the affair with Miss Marshall. He'd been aware of his father's philandering for some time, and he was deeply angered that the girl he'd introduced to the firm was now involved in what he saw as one of a series of passing affairs. When he heard about the baby, he was shattered. He began to see that it wasn't just a trivial relationship, and he too tried to persuade me to end a marriage which by then had become pretty much of a hell for all concerned.'

She looked down at her hands folded in her lap. 'But I wouldn't listen. I refused utterly to become that object of pity and derision—the middle aged deserted wife. In the end Jason told us that he wanted nothing further to do with either of us and left Tristans.' She smiled wrily. 'It seemed to me that because of this Marshall girl I had lost my husband, and now my son. I began to hate her more than I had ever thought possible. When her child was born and my husband told me he had registered the birth, stating he was the father, I behaved like a mad woman. It wasn't long after that I suffered my first mild heart attack.' She looked calmly at Laura. 'I needed a weapon, and now I had one, and I used it. I told him that while I was prepared for him to go on supporting Clare Marshall and her child, he was not to see her again. For a while, our marriage tottered on. What I hadn't foreseen of course was the breakdown in my husband's own health.'

She smiled a little. 'By this time, of course, Jason had met and married you. In spite of the breach between us, we'd kept track of him naturally. We contacted him, asked if we could meet you. The answer came back that he wouldn't bring the girl he loved to be contaminated by the kind of dishonest relationship we were practising.'

Laura who'd been sitting as if turned to marble, stirred in her chair. 'That was cruel of him,' she said slowly.

'It was justified,' Lady Wingard said drily. 'After all Jason had experienced first hand the kind of dreadful hostility and bitterness that existed between us. It was what had driven him away.'

'But when his father collapsed with a stroke, he was the one who got him into the private clinic, and there was a reconciliation of sorts. There had to be. My husband had been on the point of transferring to Miss Marshall's bank account the money she needed for herself and the child, including the rental of the flat.' She drew a deep breath. 'I'd assumed the relationship was at an end, only to discover that he'd actually been taken ill at her flat, and that she was expecting another child.'

Laura was looking back, remembering with a kind of

incredulity the conclusions she had drawn. She said, 'So Clare Marshall turned to Jason—didn't she?'

'She had little choice. The rent was due and there were other bills which in the normal course of events my husband would have settled. She had no money— and I refused to advance her any, even though I'd received a message from my husband begging me to do so. And—Jason came to her rescue.'

'The money he borrowed from our savings account.' Laura's eyes were anguished. 'Why—oh why didn't he tell me what was going on?'

'Because I had begged him not to,' Jason's mother said flatly. 'I told him it would kill me if one word of his father's infidelity ever leaked out to another soul. I even staged another attack, and I got his promise. He would never ever tell anyone the truth about his father and Miss Marshall without my agreement.' Her eyes met Laura's. 'If you're waiting to hear me say that I would have behaved differently if I'd known the harm I was going to cause, then I'm afraid you'll be disappointed, my dear. I cared for nothing but my own pride—and that image of the perfect marriage. And when my husband died, it became in some strange way, even more important to sustain the pretence.'

'Jason came to me in a terrible state. He told me you had left him, believing him to be Clare's lover and the father of her children. There was an awful scene and when he left, I didn't have to pretend any more. I became genuinely ill. They talk about kismet, don't they? Perhaps this was mine.'

'You still wouldn't let him tell the truth?' Laura's body was as taut as a bowstring.

Lady Wingard shook her head. 'All I can say in my own defence is that for a long time I was too ill even to discuss the matter. Later—gradually—I came to see what I had done, but still I couldn't bear to admit openly that my perfect marriage had been nothing but a

sham, and that the real love of my husband's life had
been a girl half his age.' She sighed. 'Jason had
inherited Tristans, and he made sure that Miss Marshall
received adequate financial provision. Death was
something my husband had never contemplated and he
had neglected to change his will in her favour.

'Jason informed me he was going to make himself
responsible for her, and I had no choice but to agree. I
knew what people would think and I welcomed it.
Anything, I thought, but the truth.

'Since my last attack I've had a lot of time to think—
to realise the unhappiness I've caused. While my son
and I were estranged, and you were just a name, it
didn't seem to matter so much that I'd contributed to
your divorce. But living with Jason, seeing his
unhappiness at first hand was another matter.'

The upright back became if possible a little
straighter. 'Even so, if Jason had been able to win
you back to him without my having to give you this
explanation, I should have been more than thankful.
It's not pleasant to have to parade one's selfishness
and malice in front of someone you are meeting for
the first time.'

There was a long pause, then she added quietly, 'I
won't ask you to forgive me, Laura, because I quite see
that may not be possible. I only ask you to understand
and make allowance for my failings.' She picked up a
small handbell from the table beside her and rang it
imperatively.

Only a few seconds later, Laura heard the door
behind her open and someone enter the room. Instinct
told her that it was not Wanda Bishop.

Lady Wingard said crisply, 'Wanda is making tea,
but I advise you, Jason, to take your wife away and
give her something stronger. She looks as if she needs
it.' She paused, then said more gently, 'I've put the
record straight—at long last. I only hope and pray that I

haven't left it too late for you both. Now, leave me
please. I need some time to collect myself.'

Laura looked up at her husband. His face was pale,
his mouth grimly set. He said quietly, 'Come with me,
Laura. We need to talk.'

They went through some french windows into the
garden. The rain had stopped, and the air was cool and
full of the fragrance of grass and wet earth.

He said, 'So now you know all of it.'

She said, on a little shaken breath, 'Yes—oh God—
yes. Jason, why didn't you tell me? Why did you let me
go on thinking all those terrible things?'

'Because I'd given mother my word,' he said grimly.
'And because the doctor told me I had to accede to her
every whim, that he couldn't answer for her life if she
had any more upsets. It was an obsession with her—this
pretence that she and my father were a devoted couple.
At times, I swear she even believed it herself. And then
she began to change, to face up to what had really
happened, and I started to hope.'

He added quietly, 'For a long time I felt pretty bitter
myself. It amazed me that you'd just accepted the fact
that I was a liar and a swine without question.' He
looked at her gravely. 'I told you once you'd never
asked me the question that mattered—asked if it was
true. What I wanted was for you to believe in me, no
matter how black the evidence might look. But the
circumstances, and your uncle's interference were too
strong for me.' He put his hands on her shoulders,
looking down into her eyes. 'What nearly killed me was
the thought that I'd lost you without ever really having
possessed you. There always seemed to be some—
reticence in you—even in our closest moments. I
thought maybe that was why you'd found it so easy to
leave me—because in your heart you preferred being on
your own.'

She said shakily, 'Finding you was like finding the

other half of myself. But it worried me that you would
never talk about yourself. Now, I can understand why,
but at the time I felt you only wanted me to share part
of your life. I knew there was something—some secret
that you wanted to keep from me, and I suppose that
was why I believed those horrible reports from the
detective agency. It all suddenly seemed to make a
dreadful kind of sense.'

He said softly, 'So many times—oh, darling—so many
times I wanted to tell you everything—pour it all out.
But you were so young—so untouched by life in many
ways that it seemed unfair to burden you with it. I
wanted you from that first moment, but told myself I
had to stay aloof. I'd seen enough of what could
happen between two people when love turned sour. It
sickened me, and I was determined I would never let it
happen—even if it meant I could never let a woman get
close to me emotionally.' He put out his hand
smoothing her hair back from her face. 'Then—after
we'd made love—I knew I'd fallen into the trap. I loved
you, and I couldn't live without you. That's why I went
away for a while—to try and persuade myself that it
was unfair to marry you when I had all these family
problems to contend with.'

She looked up at him, her eyes grave and
questioning, 'Was that why you would never say you
loved me?'

'In a way,' he said. 'It seemed to me that all I'd been
able to associate with the word "love" were lies and
deceit and bitterness. I didn't want to use it to describe
what I felt for you. But I did love you, Laura, and I've
never stopped loving you, even when we were furthest
apart.'

He put his arms around her, drawing her gently
against him. He said in a low voice, 'When the Tristan
move was first suggested, I nearly vetoed it. I was—
terrified to face you again in spite of everything, I'd

staked so much on seeing you—on there being something left. I knew I could get to see you through your uncle, but it almost killed me trying to figure what your reaction would be.' He groaned. 'If you'd treated me with indifference, as I half-expected, I think I'd have cut my throat. And when I found you were dating that pathetic creature, God, I was so jealous I could have killed him.'

She said in a small voice, 'How do you think I felt, watching you with Celia?'

He smiled wrily. 'Exactly how I wanted you to feel, darling. Why else would I have spent all those hours letting her bore me to death? She provided me with an excuse to call at the house whenever I wanted.'

'But you spent the night with her,' Laura bit her lip. 'I—I saw your car outside the house—the night we went to the restaurant—when the storm woke me.'

'The car was there, but I wasn't,' he said. 'I went for a long walk that night, going over every detail of everything you'd said and done, asking myself if I had a hope in hell of getting you back.' He grimaced. 'I remember that storm. I got drenched. At the time it seemed like divine retribution.' He stared down at her. 'Did you really think I'd slept with Celia?'

She said unhappily, 'Well, she'd made it clear from the start that she wanted you—and you were a free agent, after all. And she always talked as if you had serious intentions about her.'

'Well, she knows differently now,' he said cynically. 'Don't worry about your pretty cousin, darling. Her ego is far too armour plated to allow any real damage to be done. She was on the make for a rich husband, and I fitted the bill. But I blotted my copybook where Celia was concerned by rejecting all the palatial residences she had lined up and choosing Mill Cottage.' He paused. 'There's one thing, Laura. Wherever we live, I have to provide a home for Clare and the children.

She's been desperately lonely since my father died, which is why I brought her to live near me, but if you really can't face the arrangement . . .'

'I like her,' Laura confessed. 'I didn't want to, but I couldn't help myself?'

'I'm glad.' He bent and kissed her, his mouth tender. When he lifted his head, she said, 'Did you really ask her to marry you?'

'Yes,' he said. 'When I found out she was expecting the first child—my namesake incidentally. Half-brothers both called Jason after their father. Have you ever heard anything so ridiculous?' He paused. 'I wasn't in love with her ever, but I was fond of her and I felt guilty because I'd persuaded her to join Tristans' with me.' His lips tightened. 'I knew all about my father's habit of loving and leaving them, and it turned my stomach. I couldn't bear to think of it happening to her. But then I hadn't realised that they really loved each other.' He sighed. 'He was with her when he was taken ill, and she was the last person he mentioned before he died. He asked me to take care of her, and the boy, and their unborn child. I had to agree,' he added wrily. 'I'd already lost you, it seemed, so I felt I had nothing more to lose. And watching Clare grieve for my father was almost therapeutic. It seemed so genuine and dignified after my mother's histrionics.'

She said slowly, 'Your mother has been a very unhappy woman. I should hate her for what she did to us, but I can't—any more than I can hate Uncle Martin.'

He said drily, 'The two of them should get on well together. They're both bloody dangerous when cornered. I could hardly believe it when she agreed to tell you the truth after all this time.'

'Why do you think she did?'

He shrugged. 'Because she's a very sick woman, with not a great deal of time to make amends. Because she knew that I was going to win you back, even if it took the rest of my life, and if she wanted to go on seeing me, that was the price she had to pay. Because she thought I might get Clare to tell you the truth.'

'Why didn't you?'

He shrugged. 'Would you have believed her? I couldn't take the risk. It was essential that you hear the whole messy story from someone you would have to believe—and my mother was the only person.' His mouth twisted. 'I told her it could no longer go on being her little secret to take with her to the grave, because there was no way I was going to let her ruin my life a second time. I'd guessed ages ago you were planning to go away—I found a pile of magazines in the drawing room with advertisements marked. I realised time was running out for me, and that was when I enlisted my mother's help and set up this scheme to get you to Warwick.' He paused. 'So—when you dropped your bombshell, all I needed to do was 'phone your friend Bethany and get her on my side.' He groaned. 'My God, I thought my mother was tough.'

Laura said ruefully, 'I should have realised something wasn't right. She said such odd things—and it was all such an amazing coincidence that I should have smelled a rat, but I suppose I wasn't thinking very straight.'

He drew her close to him again. 'I'm glad you weren't. You did just what I wanted.' He raised her hands to his lips and kissed them. 'We'll go into Warwick presently and buy you another ring.'

She shook her head. 'There's no need. I didn't get rid of the first one. I couldn't bear to. It's in my bag in the house.'

'Then I'll buy you a diamond to wear with it,' he promised. He framed her face between his hands. 'The other night, after we made love, I was so happy. I looked at you lying beside me, your hair spread all over the pillow, and I remembered that other portrait of you I always meant to paint.'

She smiled, blushing a little. 'I remember too.' She quoted, ' "Laura fulfilled" ', and he nodded.

He bent his head and kissed her very slowly and sensuously, making her heart sing with excitement and joy.

He whispered, 'Will you pose for me again, my dearest love?'

She smiled up at him, her eyes alive with love, and the promise of love. 'Whenever you wish,' she said demurely. 'I have nothing else planned for the next fifty years or so.'

He said, 'Consider yourself hired.'

He kissed her fiercely, possessively and she responded with passionate eagerness, her body rejoicing in the warmth and strength of his arms around her.

Whatever the problems, from that moment on they would face them together. Neither of them would ever be alone again.

Coming Next Month in Harlequin Presents!

839 BITTER ENCORE—Helen Bianchin
Nothing can erase the memory of their shared passion. But can an estranged couple reunite when his star status still leaves no room for her in his life—except in his bed?

840 FANTASY—Emma Darcy
On a secluded beach near Sydney, a model, disillusioned by her fiancé, finds love in the arms of a stranger. Or is it all a dream—this man, this fantasy?

841 RENT-A-BRIDE LTD—Emma Goldrick
Fearful of being forced to marry her aunt's stepson, an heiress confides in a fellow passenger on her flight from Denver—never thinking he'd pass himself off as her new husband!

842 WHO'S BEEN SLEEPING IN MY BED?—Charlotte Lamb
The good-looking playwright trying to win her affection at the family villa in France asks too many questions about her father's affairs. She's sure he's using her.

843 STOLEN SUMMER—Anne Mather
She's five years older, a friend of the family's. And he's engaged! How can she take seriously a young man's amorous advances? Then again, how can she not?

844 LIGHTNING STORM—Anne McAllister
A young widow returns to California and re-encounters the man who rejected her years before—a man after a good time with no commitments. Does lightning really strike twice?

845 IMPASSE—Margaret Pargeter
Unable to live as his mistress, a woman left the man she loves. Now he desires her more than ever—enough, at least, to ruin her engagement to another man!

846 FRANGIPANI—Anne Weale
Her sister's offer to find her a millionaire before they dock in Fiji is distressing. She isn't interested. But the captain of the ship finds that hard to believe....

Here's how to get this special offer from Harlequin!
As simple as 1...2...3!

NOVEMBER
TREASURY EDITION
COUPON

1. Each month, save one Treasury Edition coupon from your favorite Romance or Presents novel.
2. In four months you'll have saved four Treasury Edition coupons (<u>only one coupon</u> per month allowed).
3. Then all you have to do is fill out and return the order form provided, along with the four Treasury Edition coupons required and $1.00 for postage and handling.

Mail to: Harlequin Reader Service

In the U.S.A.
2504 West Southern Ave.
Tempe, AZ 85282

In Canada
P.O. Box 2800, Postal Station A
5170 Yonge Street
Willowdale, Ont. M2N 6J3

RT1-D-2

Please send me my FREE copy of the Janet Dailey Treasury Edition. I have enclosed the four Treasury Edition coupons required and $1.00 for postage and handling along with this order form.

(Please Print)

NAME_____

ADDRESS_____

CITY_____

STATE/PROV._____ ZIP/POSTAL CODE_____

SIGNATURE_____

This offer is limited to one order per household.

SUPPLIES LIMITED

This special Janet Dailey offer expires January 1986.

H·A·R·L·E·Q·U·I·N

FIRST·CLASS
Sweepstakes

OFFICIAL RULES

1. **NO PURCHASE NECESSARY.** To enter, complete the official entry/order form. Be sure to indicate whether or not you wish to take advantage of our subscription offer.

2. Entry blanks have been preselected for the prizes offered. Your response will be checked to see if you are a winner. In the event that these preselected responses are not claimed, a random drawing will be held from all entries received to award not less than $150,000 in prizes. This is in addition to any free, surprise or mystery gifts which might be offered. Versions of this sweepstakes with different prizes will appear in Preview Service Mailings by Harlequin Books and their affiliates. Winners selected will receive the prize offered in their sweepstakes brochure.

3. This promotion is being conducted under the supervision of Marden-Kane, an independent judging organization. By entering the sweepstakes, each entrant accepts and agrees to be bound by these rules and the decisions of the judges, which shall be final and binding. Odds of winning in the random drawing are dependent upon the total number of entries received. Taxes, if any, are the sole responsibility of the prize winners. Prizes are nontransferable. All entries must be received by August 31, 1986.

4. The following prizes will be awarded:

   (1) Grand Prize: Rolls-Royce™ *or* $100,000 Cash!
   (Rolls-Royce being offered by permission of Rolls-Royce Motors Inc.)

   (1) Second Prize: A trip for two to Paris for 7 days/6 nights. Trip includes air transportation on the Concorde, hotel accommodations...PLUS...$5,000 spending money!

   (1) Third Prize: A luxurious Mink Coat!

5. This offer is open to residents of the U.S. and Canada, 18 years or older, except employees of Harlequin Books, its affiliates, subsidiaries, Marden-Kane and all other agencies and persons connected with conducting this sweepstakes. All Federal, State and local laws apply. Void in the province of Quebec and wherever prohibited or restricted by law. Winners will be notified by mail and may be required to execute an affidavit of eligibility and release, which must be returned within 14 days after notification. Canadian winners will be required to answer a skill-testing question. Winners consent to the use of their name, photograph and/or likeness for advertising and publicity purposes in conjunction with this and similar promotions without additional compensation. One prize per family or household.

6. For a list of our most current prize winners, send a stamped, self-addressed envelope to: WINNERS LIST, c/o Marden-Kane, P.O. Box 10404, Long Island City, New York 11101

Take 4 books & a surprise gift FREE